W9-BUV-996

BENNY & SHRIMP

Katarina Mazetti

translated by Sarah Death

PENGUIN BOOKS

PENGUIN BOOKS

Published by the Penguin Group

Penguin Group (USA) Inc., 375 Hudson Street, New York, New York 10014, U.S.A.
Penguin Group (Canada), 90 Eglinton Avenue East, Suite 700, Toronto, Ontario, Canada
M4P 2Y3 (a division of Pearson Penguin Canada Inc.) • Penguin Books Ltd, 80 Strand,
London WC2R 0RL, England • Penguin Ireland, 25 St Stephen's Green, Dublin 2, Ireland
(a division of Penguin Books Ltd) • Penguin Group (Australia), 250 Camberwell Road,
Camberwell, Victoria 3124, Australia (a division of Pearson Australia Group Pty Ltd) •
Penguin Books India Pvt Ltd, 11 Community Centre, Panchsheel Park, New Delhi –
110 017, India • Penguin Group (NZ), 67 Apollo Drive, Rosedale, North Shore 0632,
New Zealand (a division of Pearson New Zealand Ltd) • Penguin Books (South Africa)
(Pty) Ltd, 24 Sturdee Avenue, Rosebank, Johannesburg 2196, South Africa

Penguin Books Ltd, Registered Offices:
80 Strand, London WC2R 0RL, England

First published in Great Britain by Short Books 2008
Published in Penguin Books 2009

1 3 5 7 9 10 8 6 4 2

Translation copyright © Sarah Death, 2008
All rights reserved

A Pamela Dorman/Penguin Book

Originally published in Swedish by Alfabeta Bokforlag AB, Stockholm, 1998.
Copyright © Katarina Mazetti, 1998.

Publisher's Note
This is a work of fiction. Names, characters, places, and incidents either are the product of
the author's imagination or are used fictitiously, and any resemblance to actual persons, living
or dead, business establishments, events, or locales is entirely coincidental.

LIBRARY OF CONGRESS CATALOGING IN PUBLICATION DATA
Mazetti, Katarina.
[Grabben i graven bredvid. English]
Benny and Shrimp / Katarina Mazetti ; translated by Sarah Death.
p. cm.
"First published in Sweden by Alfabeta 1998."
Translated from the Swedish.
ISBN 978-0-14-311599-1
1. Man-woman relationships—Fiction.   2. Widows—Fiction.   3. Dairy farmers—Fiction.
I. Death, Sarah.   II. Title.   III. Title: Benny & Shrimp.
PT9876.23.A87B46 2009
839.73'8—dc22   2008052681

Printed in the United States of America
Set in Perpetua

BENNY & SHRIMP

+❉+❉+❉+❉+❉ +❉+❉+❉+❉+❉+❉+ ❉+❉+❉+❉+❉+❉+❉+❉

Who stands up for the dead?
Looks after their rights,
listens to their problems,
and waters their potted plants?

You'll have to be on your guard!

An aggrieved, single woman in a distinctly abnormal emotional state. Who knows what I might get up to at the next full moon?

You've read Stephen King, haven't you?

I'm sitting by my husband's grave, on a dark green bench worn smooth by use, and letting his headstone irritate me.

It's a sober little chunk of natural stone with just his name on it—"Örjan Wallin" in the plainest of plain lettering. Simple, you might even say overexplicit, just like he was. And he chose it himself, too; left instructions with the funeral director.

Just a little thing like that. I mean, he wasn't even ill.

I know exactly what message he was intending his stone to convey: Death is a Completely Natural Part of the Cycle. He was a biologist.

Thanks for that, Örjan.

I sit here on my lunch break several times a week, and always at least once at weekends. If it starts raining, I get out a plastic raincoat that folds away into a little purse. It's hideously ugly; I found it in my mother's chest of drawers.

There are lots of us with raincoats like that, in the cemetery.

I always sit here for at least an hour. Presumably in the hope of getting down to the right sort of grieving if I stick at it long enough. I'd feel better if I could feel worse, you might say. If I could sit here wringing out endless hankies without stealing constant glances at myself to check the tears were genuine.

The awful truth is, half the time, all I feel is furious with him. Bloody deserter, why couldn't you watch where you were going? And my feelings the rest of the time are, I suppose, pretty much like those of a child who had a parakeet for twelve years and then it died. There, I've said it.

I miss the constant companionship and all our daily routines. There's no one rustling the paper on the sofa beside me; no smell of coffee when I come home; the shoe rack looks like a tree in winter without all Örjan's boots and wellies.

And if I can't work out the answer to "Sun god, two letters," I have to guess it, or leave it blank.

One half of the double bed's always neat.

Nobody'd worry where I'd got to if I didn't come home because I happened to have been run over by a car.

And nobody flushes the toilet if I'm not there.

So here I am, sitting in the cemetery, missing the sound of the flush. Weird enough for you, Stephen?

There's something about cemeteries that always makes me think of some convulsive, second-rate stand-up comedian. Repression and gabbled strings of words, of course—but surely I can allow myself that? I haven't much besides my little repressions to occupy me these days.

With Örjan, at least I knew who I was. We defined each other; after all, that's what relationships between two people are for.

Who am I now?

I'm at the mercy of whoever happens to see me. For some I'm a voter, for others a pedestrian, a wage earner, a consumer of culture, a human resource, or a property owner.

Or just a collection of split ends, leaking sanitary napkins, and dry skin.

Though of course I can still use Örjan for defining myself. He can do me that one, posthumous favor. If Örjan hadn't existed, I could be calling myself a "single girl, thirty-something"; I saw that in a newspaper yesterday, and it made my hair stand on end. Instead, I'm a "young, childless widow," so tragic, so very sad. Well, thanks for that, Örjan!

Somewhere there's a nagging little feeling of pure deflation, as well. I feel let down that Örjan went and died.

When we'd planned our future, short and long term! A canoeing holiday in Värmland, and a high-yield pension scheme apiece.

Örjan should be feeling let down, too. All that tai chi, organic potato, and polyunsaturated fat. What good did it do him?

Sometimes I'm outraged on his behalf. It's not fair, Örjan! When you were so well-meaning and competent!

And there's an excited little flutter between my legs now and then, after five months of celibacy. It makes me worry I've got necrophiliac tendencies.

Next to Örjan's stone there's a really tasteless gravestone, an absolute monstrosity. White marble with swirly
gold lettering; angels, roses, birds, words on garlands of
ribbon, even a salutary little skull and scythe. The grave
itself is as crowded with plants as a garden center. On the
headstone are a man's name and a woman's name with sim-
ilar dates of birth, so it must be a child honoring his father
and mother in that overlavish way.

A few weeks ago I saw the bereaved by the monstrosity
for the first time. He was a man of about my age, in a
loud, quilted jacket and a padded cap with earflaps. Its peak
went up at the front, American-style, and had a logo saying
FOREST OWNERS' ALLIANCE. He was eagerly raking
and digging his little plot.

There's nothing growing around Örjan's stone. He'd
probably have thought a little rosebush totally out of keeping, since it wasn't a species native to the cemetery's
biotope. And they don't sell yarrow or meadowsweet in the
flower shop at the cemetery gates.

The Forest Owner comes regularly every few days,
about noon. He's always loaded down with new plants and
fertilizers. He seems to take great pride in his gardening, as
if the grave were his allotment.

Last time, he sat down on the seat beside me and looked
at me sideways, but he didn't say anything.

He had a funny smell and only three fingers on his left
hand.

Damn and blast! I can't stand her, just can't stand the sight of her!

Why's she always sitting there?

I used to sit on the bench for a little while after I'd done the grave, and finish thinking all my interrupted thoughts, hoping to find a loose end to grab onto, to keep me plodding on through the next day or two. If I don't keep my mind on the job, there's inevitably some little disaster and I have to spend an extra day sorting it out. Like I run the tractor into a rock and break the back axle. Or a cow tramples one of her teats because I forgot to fix on her bra—I mean udder guard.

Going to the grave is my only breathing space, and even then I never feel I can just sit there thinking. I have to rake and plant and weed before I can let myself sit down.

And then she's there.

Faded, like some old color photo that's been on display for years. Dried-out blond hair, a pale face, white eyebrows and lashes, wishy-washy pastel clothes, always something vaguely blue or beige. A beige person. The total insolence of her—it would only take a bit of makeup or bright jewelry to let the people around her know that here's someone who at least cares what you see and what you think of me. All her paleness says is: I don't give a damn what you think; I don't so much as notice you.

I like a woman's appearance to say: look at me, see what I've got to offer! It makes me feel sort of flattered. She should have shiny lipstick and little shoes with straps and pointed toes, and her breasts boosted up under your nose. It doesn't matter if her lipstick's a bit smudged, or her dress pulls tight over her spare tire, or there's hardly room for all her huge artificial pearls—not everybody can have good taste; it's making the effort that counts. I always fall a little bit in love when I see a woman who's not all that young any more but who's invested half a day's work in getting noticed, especially if she's got long, false nails, hair permed to extinction, and teetering high heels. It makes me want to hold her and cuddle her and pay her compliments.

I never do, of course. I never get nearer than watching them in the post office or the bank; there are no women on the farm except the inseminator and the vet. In long, blue rubber aprons, big boots, scarves tied around their hair, dashing in with a test tube of bull's semen. And they never have time to stay for a cup of coffee—even assuming I'd had time to go in and make one.

Mum used to nag me in those last years to "go out" and find myself a girl. As if they existed somewhere, a flock of willing girls, and all you had to do was go out and select one. Like taking your rifle out in the hunting season to bag yourself a hare.

Because she knew, long before I did, that the cancer was

slowly eating her from inside and I'd be left on my own. Not just with all the outdoor work to do, but also the many other things she'd provided over the years: a warm house, a freshly changed bed, clean overalls every other day, nice food, constant hot coffee with homemade buns. Backed up by all those jobs I'd never had to think about—chopping firewood, stoking the boiler, picking berries, doing the washing; all those things I don't find time for now. Overalls stiff with cow shit and sour milk, gray sheets, the house cold whenever you come in, Nescafé stirred into a cup of hot water from the tap. And the jumbo sausage that splits in the microwave every bloody day.

She used to leave the family section of the *Farmer* open at the personal page beside my coffee. Sometimes she'd circle one of the ads. But of course, she never said anything outright.

What Mum didn't know was that there are no young maids flocking around the milk churn platform any more, eager to keep house for Eligible Bachelor With Own Farm. They all disappeared off to town some years back and now they're nursery school teachers and junior nurses and married to car mechanics and salesmen and thinking about buying a little house. Sometimes in the summer they come back here with their partner and some flaxen-haired bundle in a baby carrier, to laze on their backs in deck chairs outside their parents' old farms for a few weeks.

Carina, who was always after me in upper secondary school and could be persuaded to do it if you chatted her up a bit, ambushes me now and then from behind the shelves in the shop. The shop's still open in summer; it might be good for a few more years. Suddenly she'll jump out and pretend it's a coincidence and start interrogating me about whether I'm married or have got any children. She lives in town now, with Stefan, who works as a cashier for the Co-op, she says triumphantly, looking as if she expects me to burst into tears at what I've missed out on. Like hell.

Maybe she, the pale woman, has parents to visit and laze on her back with in summer. It'd be nice to be rid of her for a few weeks. Though in summer there's no time to come here, not unless it pours with rain one day and stops me from getting on with the haymaking.

And that gravestone she sits staring at! What sort of a stone do you call that? It looks like something a surveyor put down as a boundary marker!

Mum chose Dad's headstone; I can see it's garish but I can also see all the love that went into choosing it. She spent several weeks, ordered catalogues and everything. Every day she had some new idea for the design and in the end she went for the whole lot.

Örjan, is that her father, or a brother, or her bloke? And if she can bring herself to come here and sit staring at that stone day after day, why can't she bring herself to put even one flowering plant on the grave?

Of course the edges of the wound struggle to close up
and the clock wants to be set going
(how awkward to be pointing permanently to half past one)—
amputated limbs feel phantom pain

Something utterly unexpected happened today.

It was a clear, cold autumn day and I took my usual walk to the grave on my lunch break. The Forest Owner was sitting there on the bench; he glowered at me, as if I were trespassing in his own private cemetery. His paws were all soily; he'd probably just got the day's gardening stint out of the way. Wonder why he's only got three fingers.

I sat down on the seat and started brooding about how many children Örjan and I would have had. Örjan would have taken his full share of paternity leave and been an expert on terry cloth diapers and practical child carriers. Taken the baby to swimming classes.

We were married for five years and in all that time we hardly argued. There was the occasional abrupt comment, the odd sarcastic remark or irritated snort. Always from my side, but it never escalated.

No thanks to me. Örjan never argued with anybody.

He patiently explained his point of view over and over again until you were forced to give in from sheer exhaustion.

There were a few times when his mild-mannered nature just made me lose control. I'd start having a childish tantrum—kicking the furniture, stomping out of the room, slamming the door. He always behaved as if he hadn't noticed, and I didn't keep it up because it just felt as if I was conceding him points for style.

Once I scrunched up the paper page by page and bombarded him with balls of newspaper. We'd spent half of Saturday on the paper—debating the controversial articles; noting cultural events even if they were happening hundreds of miles away; laughing at the comic strips and planning a tasty Saturday supper with sundried tomatoes. I had a sudden feeling real life was passing me by, rushing past outside the window while we sat there reading, and I grabbed the paper and went on the attack. Then his brown eyes filled with such concern that I was left with no choice but to hit him or burst into tears.

So I cried, of course, furiously. Because the provoking thing was, he was the one most likely to pull on his green wellies and go out into the real world, birdwatching binoculars in hand, before I'd even got to the review section of the paper. "You've always got to have a lens between you and reality," I snuffled, feeling more misunderstood than ever, since I didn't even understand myself.

A few days later, studiedly casual, he handed me an article about premenstrual tension and gave me such a kindly pat on the hand, which immediately made me want to scrunch that into a ball and throw it at him. But before I could move, he'd unlocked his mountain bike out in the courtyard and disappeared.

In the beginning I was in love with him. I wrote love letters in hexameters, which made him smile. I climbed out on creaking branches to photograph birds' nests for him and stood in ice-cold water letting leeches attach themselves to my legs because he needed them for research.

Maybe it was because he was so good-looking. Warm, brown coloring; tall, well-built body; lovely, muscular hands always busy with something. It felt good to see other women sneaking a look at him and then gulping in amazement when they saw my washed-out figure at his side. (Oh yes, girls! I landed this catch all by myself and I could teach you a thing or two!)

An empty boast. I've no idea how I "got" him. Good-looking men don't normally show any more interest in me than they would in a wallpaper design selected by the council housing department.

But once Örjan had me in his sights—I worked at the information desk in the library and helped him with zoology periodicals in English—he seemed to decide that I was definitely His Woman, the only one he would do any favors for from now on. Rather as he always favored buying Fjällräven's outdoor gear.

At the beginning I felt as if he was checking me out, like some kind of all-embracing consumer test. In the woods. In bed. At the cinema, then chatting in the café afterward. And there were no sharp corners anywhere. We stitched all our opinions neatly into each other like two knitting needles in the same bit of knitting, and happily watched the pattern starting to build up.

Then we got married and recovered our breath. Examination successfully passed, time for the next phase.

We'd just started exchanging smiles in front of the

11

window of the stroller shop when he went and died. He was run over by a truck early one morning, on his bike on his way to watch the mating display of the capercaillie. He was listening to a tape of birdcalls on his headphones—either he didn't hear the truck and veered out in front of it, or the driver fell asleep at the wheel.

This sober little stone in front of me is all I've got left. And I'm furious with him for leaving me like that, without even discussing it first. . . . Now I'll never find out who he was.

I got my notebook out of my bag. It's a little blue book with stiff covers and a bright blue sailing boat on the front. And I wrote:

> *Of course the edges of the wound struggle to close up*
> *and the clock wants to be set going*

I honestly don't imagine that what I'm doing in my notebook is creating Poetry. I'm just trying to capture existence in images. I do that most days, rather as other people write to-do lists to impose some order on their daily lives. No one need ever read them—I don't tell other people my dreams, either. Everyone has their own method for getting a grip on life.

The Forest Owner was watching me furtively from the side. You stare if you like, I thought, and it's fine by me if you think I'm Organized Housewife doing her weekly budget.

Just as I was unscrewing the top of my fountain pen (I've managed to get hold of one—when you're putting your thoughts into words, it has to be in proper ink), a mother came along with a little girl of about three or four trotting beside her to the grave on the other side of the Forest Owner's. The girl had a shiny little watering can, which was bright pink and looked brand new, and she was carrying it as if it were the crown jewels. The mother began to busy herself with tapering vases and bouquets in rustling paper, while the girl skipped around the gravestone pouring dribbles of water from her can. Suddenly she clapped her hand over her mouth; she looked petrified, her eyes as round as marbles: "Oh, Mummy! I watered the writing! Now Grandpa will be really cross, won't he?"

I felt the corners of my mouth twitch and threw a glance at the Forest Owner. And at the same instant, he looked at me.

He smiled, too. And . . .

There's no way of describing that smile without resorting to the wonderful world of cheesy song lyrics.

It had sun and wild strawberries and birds singing and expanses of glittering water in it. And it was directed at me, trusting and proud as if he were a child presenting me with a misshapen birthday gift. The corners of my mouth were still stretched wide. And an arc of light flashed between us, I'd still swear it even today—a blue one like my physics teacher could produce with that special generator thing of his. Three hours passed, or maybe three seconds.

Then we turned our heads to face the front, simultaneously, as if we were both being operated by the same string. The sun went behind the clouds and I just sat there, replaying his smile in slow motion behind my eyelids.

If Märta, my best or possibly only friend Märta, had told

me about a smile like the one the Forest Owner and I had just exchanged, I'd have thought she was showing her usual capacity for rewriting reality into something bigger and more beautiful.

I envy her for it. My own tendency is to think that a baby's smile is just wind; a falling star is very likely a TV satellite crashing out of orbit; birdsong is full of territorial threats; and Jesus probably never existed, at least not then and not there.

"Love" is how a species answers the need for genetic variation, otherwise you could easily just take cuttings from the females.

Of course I know there are strong forces operating between men and women. Your egg is sloshing around in there wanting nothing better than to be fertilized by some suitable sperm. The whole machinery jolts into action whenever any of it comes within reach.

But what I wasn't prepared for was the sperm container smiling like that! The egg did a leap inside me, jumping and splashing and turning somersaults and sending out frantic signals, "This way! This way!"

I wanted to shout to it, "Sit!"

I turned my head so I was looking away from the Forest Owner and instead peered furtively at his hand on the bench. He was twisting a Volvo keyring between his two fingers and thumb. Where his ring finger and his little finger should have been, there were just smooth knuckles. His hands were ingrained with earth and perhaps oil, and the veins stood out on the back of them. I wanted to smell his hands and caress the empty knuckles with my lips.

Good God, I've got to get away from here! Is this what

happens to a grown-up woman who lives without a man for a while?

So I stood up, grabbed up my bag in my cold hands, and ran, taking the most direct route to the gates, across graves and low hedges.

I'm way behind with the accounts. It feels as if everything's going to the dogs; wonder if that's why I've put off getting down to the bills and paperwork. The piles of paper spilling out from Dad's old desk feel explosive, as if there's some bloody letter from the bank sitting ticking in there, a letter telling me I'm scraping the bottom of my loan arrangement. I scarcely dare answer the phone during office hours any more; it might be them.

I've never been any good with money, or paperwork. That was Mum's forte. She used to sit there at the desk muttering under her breath; now and then she'd turn around and look at me across one sidepiece of her glasses and ask some question that only needed a straightforward answer: "Are we all right for seed? Have you paid the vet?"

She took care of everything else. And all I had to do was tell her how much cash I needed; she never asked questions, not even when I took it into my head to buy a wide gold bracelet for Annette, who I was with for a while.

Annette was always going on about how much she liked Bismarck chains—that's almost the only thing I remember about her.

Mum said once, near the end, that I ought to call in the Farm Management Service to take care of all that now. She lay there thinking about things like that, although she had a drip in her arm. The drip meant she kept needing bedpans, and she found it really embarrassing. I always said I was going out for a smoke when the nurse brought the bedpan in. And I hadn't the heart to tell her I wouldn't be able to afford the Farm Management Service; the milk check seemed to be shrinking every month.

In any case, it's not called the Farm Management Service any more, and they employ all those slick young stock-broker types there nowadays. Just being in their office makes me feel uncomfortable.

Mum's overriding feeling seemed to be one of frustration with her cancer for stopping her from getting up and doing anything useful. The chemotherapy really knocked her out, but whenever I came in, the impression she gave was along the lines of: "What a wretched nuisance. It's too bad! I'm afraid you'll have to excuse me."

Oh hell, she's back, the beige woman! Hasn't she anything better to do? She looks like someone who still lives at home with her parents, with some nice little job while she waits to marry the bank manager. She blasted well looks as if she might work at my bank.

She sits down and gives me a sideways look, as if I were a bouncing check—an embarrassment, but not her problem. Then she sighs deeply and gets some kind of writing book out of a big flowery bag. She makes a great performance of taking the top off a pen—a fountain pen?

I didn't think anyone used those since ballpoints were invented—and starts writing, slowly and in spidery little handwriting.

And, of course, I'm itching with curiosity. Who is this woman making notes by a grave? Does she keep a record of all the husbands she's finished off? Suddenly she frowns and I hear a distinct, abrupt snort: she'd noticed I was sitting looking at her. To pay her back for her snooty attitude I try to picture her with fishnet stockings and a curly mauve nylon wig. Flour-white breasts, firmly clamped into a deep cleavage and bulging out of a tight-laced patent-leather corset. I let her keep the white eyelashes and the stupid hairy wool hat with the toadstools on it.

The image I've conjured up is so ridiculous that I suddenly find I'm sitting staring at her, grinning from ear to ear. She gives me another look and—before I can rearrange my features, she's smiling back!

Can this really be her? The beige woman, who sits worshipping a chunk of old granite and pursing her pale lips, can she smile like this?

Like a child in the summer holidays, or a kid that's just got its first bike? The same happy, all-over grin as that little girl with the pink watering can over there by the other grave.

We're stuck like that. We've both got our headlights on full beam and neither of us is giving way.

What the hell's going on here?

Should I do something? Say, "Do you come here often? Busy in the cemetery today, isn't it? What do you think of the chapel?" Or start pressing my knee against hers.

Then someone pulls the plug and we're both staring straight ahead.

We sit there for a bit, stock-still as if the bench were

mined. Then I start fiddling with my keys to stop myself from exploding into little bits.

I can see out of the corner of my eye that she's transfixed by my hand and trying not to show it. I've been practicing for years not hiding it in my pocket as soon as people start staring. And I don't now, either. Three-Finger Benny, that's me, babe. Take it or leave it!

Ha, it turned out to be "leave it." She gets up and stumbles off as if I'd been planning to grab her with my pathetic threesome. Why's she looking so angry?

Yet another conquest for Smarmy Benny, I guess.

That was how things always turned out in the days when I was forever on the lookout for girls. I went the way my prick told me, and it always led me to girls, like a divining rod; all I had to do was hang on and follow it. To open-air dances in the summer; to some place where there was a dance in the winter, even if it was sometimes a long journey. Big, dreary halls with fluorescent strip lighting, used by the local school for gym in the daytime and by the temperance society for meetings in the evening, and then on Fridays and Saturdays they'd put some crepe paper around the lights and bring in a dance band. I hardly ever drove into town to go to these parties, partly because I knew I'd lost touch with modern trends—I realized that when people started wearing their caps back to front—but also because to me there seemed no point in standing apart and jiggling about. I wanted someone to hold. I thought it was great putting my arm around the waist of a new girl and steering her out onto the dance floor; it was like buying a raffle ticket and winning every time. They smelled so nice and I thought they were all so pretty. I was in love with every single one and didn't want to let go of them when the dance was over. And I definitely didn't want to try to speak over the band and have a conversation with them or anything. I just wanted to hold them and smell them and glide around with my eyes closed.

It never occurred to me that I couldn't just take what I wanted—the last year at school I'd been one of those boys loads of girls fancied; my name was written on girls' desks all over the place. But I hadn't seen many girls since I took over the farm, and you don't notice the years passing. I hadn't realized how out of practice I was.

It all went well to start with. I traipsed around as the fancy took me, and most girls are good at keeping their feet out of the way. Sometimes they were better than that; they had such an irresistible way of moving in time to the music that we seemed to be dancing automatically, and that was great. When the dance finished, they started giving me sideways looks, and I'd stand there staring at them, smiling, never saying "Do you come here often . . . ? What do you think of the band . . . ? Busy here tonight . . . ," like you're supposed to. I've nothing against small talk, it keeps the friendly mood going, but it just isn't my sort of thing. Some of the girls broke off after a couple of dances and went back to their place—the girls always stood in a gaggle by one particular wall. But most of them carried on dancing.

Once I opened my mouth and said to a girl, "What makes you happy?"

I'd been sort of wondering about it as we danced.

"Makes me what?" she shouted over all the noise.

"Happy! What makes you . . . Oh heck, forget it!" I swiftly deposited her back with the gaggle of girls, my ears red.

But that wasn't the worst thing. Once I blithely danced

five dances in a row with a girl; she smelled so nice. After the fifth dance, I leaned forward and nuzzled her in the neck without even thinking.

She instantly took three steps back. Did she think I was a vampire? In my mind's eye I saw my wimpish, fluoride-enhanced fangs growing long and pointed and couldn't help smiling broadly. At that she hissed like an angry swan, turned on her heel, and left me there.

Later I happened to be standing behind her in the entrance hall. "What did that smarmy guy think he was doing?" her friend asked. "He must have been drunk," she said. "Didn't say a word, just grinned like an idiot."

Smarmy guy. A name that conjures up the impression of silk shirts and too much aftershave. Somebody trying too hard.

Smarmy Benny. Frightens people into bolting with his killer smile. Expect that was why she ran, too, the beige woman.

But, well . . . she was smiling, wasn't she?

Day after day,
face to face
with broken mirrors
and vindictive meter maids

Reading the jottings in my blue book from that autumn, it strikes me that maybe I was depressed, in the clinical sense of the word.

At work I'd joke almost hysterically in the staff room, and relish seeing people laugh until their mascara ran. Everything would suddenly feel normal then, and I'd be the one enjoying it all most.

And when I got home with my Co-op carrier bag at the end of the afternoon, I always made sure I had plenty to keep me occupied. I arranged the vegetables I'd just bought into a still life on a ceramic dish from Denmark, watered my sprouting seeds, carefully selected some suitably wild opera aria to play at top volume, lit candles in the bathroom, and took long baths as the lavender scent of the aroma-therapy lamp slowly filled the white room.

That autumn I read autobiographies and whole series of

fantasy fiction; at best they had a narcotic effect—like stepping into other worlds. And when they suddenly came to an end, I would lie back at one end of the sofa, weak and trembling, as if washed ashore on a beach after a shipwreck. The biographies and the fantasy worlds asked me: Why are you alive, and what are you making of this life, so fragile, so unwieldy and short?

At night I dreamed a variety of answers. In one of the dreams I was a goddess, moving through a latticework of shadows and light, and my fingertips sprouted life in different forms: luxuriant, fleshy creepers and plump children's bodies.

Other days seemed mostly to consist of sleet and eternal waits for the bus. I increased my pension contributions, made a will, and left instructions for my funeral—if Örjan had chosen that funeral director, the least I could do was follow his lead. On days like those I sorted receipts into separate folders, bought IKEA storage boxes to stack in the wardrobe, and started putting old photos in frames—the pictures held no more significance than the last year's dead, rustling leaves.

I'd often masturbate. The men in my fantasies were all strapping types with rough chins and callused hands. They had no faces above chin level.

Märta was my life preserver, my anchor in life. She might come charging in, right into the bathroom, waving two cinema tickets until I dragged myself upright, blew out the candles in the candelabra, and went with her. Afterward we'd come back to my place, take a sofa each, and review the details of our daily grind and the meaning of life in one glorious mix, from her neurotic boss's latest tricks to an impassioned critique of St. Augustine's views on women.

Märta exuded a warm scent of bread, eau de parfum, and cigarillos. She lived intermittently with Robert, her Greatest Passion, and sometimes when he was away on one of his mysterious business trips, Märta and I would drink a bottle of white port between us and then she'd spend the night on my sofa. We'd devote the following morning to peaceable, low-level bickering, with lank hair and bags under our eyes. Märta in Örjan's drab bathrobe that I couldn't bring myself to get rid of. More than once we bemoaned the fact that we weren't lesbians—I could imagine myself living with someone like her, and she often found Robert more than she could bear.

One night I told her about the Forest Owner and the inexplicable smile. She sat upright on the sofa, licked her index finger, and held it up to test the way the wind was blowing.

"There's something in the air!" she said delightedly.

A solitary life—without family or children—maybe it means more to you if you happen to be a farmer with a fair few acres of arable land and some forest.

Who are you planting the trees for, those trees that take thirty years to be mature enough for felling? Who are you letting that land lie fallow for, so it won't be drained of nutrients and suffer long-term damage?

And who will there be to help me get the hay harvest in?

I tried to focus on the monthly milk test results. Better figures every time, higher yield, and fewer bacteria. I planned improvements to the manure system, freshened up the milking parlor, and got a new tank. I bought a new tractor with tandem mounting, not because I really needed one, but because I wanted to convince myself that at least something in my life was changing for the better.

However nonsensical it may sound, I stayed out working around the farm later and later each evening. I was reluctant to face the concentrated, empty silence of the house. It had a faint smell of decay and discomfort so one day in the middle of the week I drove into town and bought a black, cigar-shaped monster radio and stood it on the kitchen counter.

From then on, the first thing I did when I got in in the evenings, before I got under the shower, was to turn on one of the commercial stations at top volume. The excited voices pouring out of the radio gave me the feeling that at least life was going on somewhere, and a little trickle of it found its way into my shabby old kitchen. But I still couldn't bring myself to chuck out the old brown Bakelite radio with the yellowish fabric front that Dad had bought Mum for one of their wedding anniversaries in the fifties—sometimes I even had it on with the volume turned down, because the cat liked lying on it when it warmed up.

I put all my clothes in the same wash; everything turned a grayish shade of blue. Now and then I might happen to browse through the family section of the *Farmer* and see people putting up front porches with fancy carved wood-work or stuffing their own sausages. Who the hell cared what the front porch looked like? It was just a place to kick off your boots and store empty beer crates! As for sausage, you bought it in two seconds flat on your weekly trip around the Co-op.

I had vague ideas of clearing out the old fridge. There were things in there that probably could have walked out on their own. There were jars of jam with Mum's handwrit-ten labels and a thick furring of mold on top. Throwing them out would be like throwing her out.

Of course, it would have been perfectly feasible to go

along to some evening classes and Meet People. Our branch of the National Farmers' Union was running a study group on the subject "Make your farm earn," but of course, it instantly became known as "Make your farm burn," since that seemed the most profitable option. I went along to the first few sessions and met exactly the same people I usually meet at the agricultural supplier's, at Göte Nilsson Tractors, and the union's Christmas party.

At the party, though, they had their wives with them, and I'd dance with them and let my hand wander all over the place. That sometimes made some of the wives start breathing heavily and gyrating their pelvises, making me glance self-consciously in their husbands' direction. Later on in the evening, when we men had gone around the back to have a few swigs of what we'd brought with us, we told jokes about the farmer's daughter and the traveling salesman, and what the milkmaid said to the farmhand. Sometimes we got sentimental and said we were the ones holding the land in trust, and getting nothing but shit for it.

Then the party would be over and the married couples would dance the last dance with each other while the rest of us stood around the doorway arguing about slurry or the EU; and then there'd always be one with a sober wife who had to get up for an early shift at the hospital, and they'd give me a lift home. And if I wasn't too drunk I'd fantasize about one of the women I'd been holding close, and all the time it'd be in the back of my mind that I had to be up again at six, because I couldn't afford to get in a relief worker.

Now they're off home, the lot of them, to their blasted front porches with fancy woodwork, to tuck in their sleeping kids, I thought, and in the morning she'll brew him strong coffee to help him get going and then put some dough to rise and stuff some sausages. What the hell am I living for?

I'm not ashamed to admit I even wrote away to one of those mail-order bride agencies to ask them to send me a Filipino woman on approval. But when I got their brochure, scruffy photocopied pages with smudged black and white photos, it turned my stomach. I suddenly wondered what the beige woman in the cemetery would think if she could see me thumbing through that brochure. I've never felt more down in my life.

✥✖✦✖✦✖✦✖ ✦✖✦✖✦✖✦✖✦✖✦✖✦✖ ✦✖✦✖✦✖✦✖

Parking meters
best-before dates
payment deadlines
metastases from the social body

I went through a phase of feeling reluctant to go to Örjan's grave. It's getting colder, I told myself; you can't sit there letting yourself get inflammation of the ovaries. We'll risk it, said the ovaries. We fancy another look at that Forest Owner.

One day I simply got up in the middle of a meeting about the annual library budget and headed for the cemetery.

Naturally the Forest Owner wasn't there. And anyway, I wasn't at all sure I'd recognize him again if he was wearing different clothes and looking serious.

The smile, on the other hand, I'd have recognized that. Absolutely anywhere.

I felt so sorry for Örjan, my brown, handsome, well-meaning Örjan. Fancy having someone sitting at your graveside and thinking about other things. Though if I'd

29

been the one lying in the ground and Örjan the one sitting here, I bet he'd have had his binoculars with him.

My being madly in love with him was over even before we got married. It faded like a suntan—who notices when that happens? But unlike the suntan, it never came back. And there were periods before the wedding when I'd agonize over the thought of the wide blue yonder I'd never see, or at least, not with Örjan.

I asked a lot of Märta around that time. Buckets of tea until half past three in the morning.

"I mean, you can't be madly in love all your life, can you? Passion gradually changes into Love, into something more substantial to build on, doesn't it? The sort of Love that's like a warm friendship, plus sex," I whined. Good grief, I'm surprised she didn't throw up in my lap! She kept books of advice on Love Problems in the bathroom, so you could tear a page out if you needed one in an emergency.

"Hard work convincing yourself, eh?" was all she said, unconcerned, and glowered at me over her eternal cigarillos. Märta stuck to the principle of Listen to your Heart.

"Örjan's got everything," I said stubbornly.

"According to consumer research, you mean?" snorted Märta. "Best in test, sifted out from all men in the 25–35 age group? Does he really exist, or is he just a prototype? Have you checked to see if he runs on batteries? You know, if you can hear a faint hum coming from his ear . . ."

Shortly after that, Robert, her Greatest Passion, sold her car and used the money to go off to Madagascar without her. Märta's face took a serious tumble at that point, but she regained her poise by hating him, shedding the odd tear, working like crazy, and then hating him a bit more before bedtime. And when he came back, tanned and gorgeous, she opened her arms to him again within three weeks.

That did it as far as I was concerned. If that was what the wide blue yonder had in store, you could keep it.

So I embarked on the project of being Happily Married. Within six months, we had a marriage as comfy as a pair of old slippers. We were in complete agreement about equal division of the bills and the chores; gave parties for people from work, with bottles of Greek Demestica and proper Bulgarian feta; renovated furniture we found at auctions with a lick of paint; and cut interesting articles out of the newspapers for each other.

What went on between us in the double bed was a little problematic and we tended to blame that on my sensually deprived childhood. Örjan did his best with the foreplay, which never took less than half an hour, but I stayed as dry as coarse-grade sandpaper; we positively grated on each other.

Of course, I never really knew Örjan.

Not that he tried to conceal anything—if I asked, he was happy to tell me whatever I wanted to know, from his political views to his mother's maiden name. But . . .

"The people in the picture have no connection with the article," you sometimes read in the paper. That was Örjan in a nutshell, in some indefinable way. So I stopped asking.

He didn't ask much, either, and if he did, his face had "This is Me Taking an Interest" written all over it. So I stopped answering. It didn't really seem to bother him.

What seemed to bring us closest was talking about friends and acquaintances who had got divorced after stormy marriage guidance sessions. We loved sitting there going over all their mistakes, and sometimes we'd even get straight under our designer duvets and find I grated less than usual.

But my egg never, ever, turned somersaults, however hard Örjan worked on my erogenous zones.

The cemetery bench was freezing my backside off, so I got up and went. No Forest Owner today, ha! He wasn't there on my next two visits, either.

The third time, I passed him coming in at the cemetery gate as I was on my way out. He was carrying some fir twigs, a little wreath with plastic lilies, and a grave light. Of course, it was All Saints! He gave me a nod as stern as an old schoolmaster's, as if he was thinking: Well? Is your grave light properly positioned, young lady?

I thought of Märta and her Greatest Passion. Was this how it started? With finding yourself going places you didn't want to go, your feet and ovaries starting to live a life of their own?

A wreath with plastic flowers! Örjan would have found that very funny—yes, Örjan could laugh!

I didn't go to the cemetery the following week. My feet and ovaries needed putting in their place; anything else would be plain ridiculous.

Olof, who's the head librarian and recently divorced, asked me if I felt like going out for something to eat after work. We went to a new pub, with the sort of interior design no real British pub has had since the thirties. Olof's got a boyish fringe with a sprinkling of gray hairs, which falls down over his eyes when he gets enthusiastic about something, and long white hands with which he makes elegant gestures. I think it's a habit he got into when he studied at the Sorbonne in his youth.

32

We had kebabs, I drank wine, and Olof had a cloudy Belgian beer that made him wax lyrical and toss his fringe. Then we discussed Lacan and Kristeva and Gregorian chants and after that we went back to my place and made love. It was quite okay, really; I'd gone without for so long.

But my ovaries didn't sit up and take notice that time, either.

When we'd got up and showered and finished off my Pernod, he showed me photos of his two children and told me in great detail about the brace his daughter had on her teeth. Then he cried. I think we were both relieved when he left.

This was followed by several days when I didn't think about the Forest Owner. That's obviously what you have to do to put your ovaries in their place. You take an occasional lover at bedtime to keep the system ticking over. My interest in the Forest Owner was just a symptom of some deficiency, a bit like brittle nails indicating a shortage of vitamin B. A few yeast tablets, and everything's right again.

I'm a loser, in fact, the Prize Loser of all Sweden. I shall end up in the Folk Museum in Stockholm, stuffed. I'm aware of it every time I go into town, and pretty often in between as well, like when I'm watching television. I've got no business being in the twentieth century, at least, not this end of it. And that applies to my image as well as to my way of thinking.

I'm from the country and go around dressed in a random selection of gear I ordered from the Halén's catalogue. Thirty-six, that means I'm on the shelf by our village's standards. The women seldom spare me an extra glance. Things have gone downhill in a big way since I was the best javelin thrower in the school . . . twenty years ago! My God, where did those years go? A quarter of my life's passed me by while my nose has been buried in the milking records!

But it's not just my clothes that make me a loser; there

are plenty of people here in the country who dress like me, and are quite happy looking like that. It's more a case of feeling increasingly often that I must be a bit dim, to put it mildly. No common sense. Suppose I've spent too long with just the cows for company.

Take the day before yesterday, for example. It was All Saints' Day. Every All Saints' Day since Dad died, when I was seventeen, Mum and I would go to the cemetery to light a little grave light. Mum always bought a wreath with plastic pinecones or lilies, so it would stay looking nice, because we were too busy to get to the cemetery very often. Now she was lying there, and I wanted her to have a wreath like that, too.

At the cemetery gates I ran into the beige woman. I thought she'd be looking at me warily, afraid Smarmy Benny might fire off his lunatic smile at her again, so I knitted my brow and gave a curt nod as I passed her.

And then.

It was as if someone had punched me between the eyes.

I felt disappointed she was going! For several weeks I'd been telling myself it was nice to have the bench to myself and sit there meditating. But now I wanted her there beside me. I wanted to know where she went when she wasn't in the cemetery.

I turned around and followed her at a distance. People looked startled to see me lumbering along clutching a wreath and a grave light, especially as I crouched down behind parked vehicles every now and then, afraid she was about to turn around.

But she didn't. She walked briskly halfway across town and into the library.

Didn't I just know it! She looked like somebody who reads books all the time, voluntarily. Long ones, with small print and no pictures.

I hovered indecisively at the entrance. Even the Prize Loser of all Sweden realized you don't just waltz into the library brandishing a wreath and a grave light. I had a vision of myself putting the wreath on the hat rack and depositing the grave light on the circulation desk while I asked at the information counter whether they'd seen a beige girl.

Maybe she'd come out again in a minute with a bulging bag of books, her daily ration. But how long should I wait? People were already starting to give me strange stares. The Prize Loser responded with his best Smarmy Benny smile, politely waving his grave light. Don't mind me, I'm on day release from the asylum!

I suddenly turned on my heels and started running back through the town to the cemetery.

And, of course, that made people stare all the more.

Where's he off to with a wreath in such a hurry? What's happened, what's happened? And where's the corpse?

Wretched woman!

✛✖✛✖✛✖✛✖ ✛✖✛✖✛✖✛✖✛✖✛✖✛✖✛✖ ✛✖✛✖✛✖✛

I dream of a scent of apple blossom—
you stagger beneath heavy baskets.
Which of us knows anything of the apples?

"It's all right for you," said Lilian pointedly. She's one of my colleagues at the library, the one I always try to avoid when she comes steaming past with self-important, tip-tapping heels, arms full of nothing in particular, which she carries to and fro with an air of great concentration. She's always exhausted, rarely gets anything done and takes great care to ensure nobody else is secretly enjoying their job.

"Of course," she sighed, twisting her Kenzo scarf into a rope. "I mean, you can arrange to be available in the evenings and so on. You can put your job first."

She said it with a sort of aggressive insinuation that I was somehow cheating. Grown up but with no family, a black sheep in the lives of women.

Bitch! She was the one who was in the habit of putting her head to one side and asking me, "since you haven't got a family," to do her evening and Sunday shifts for her.

I'd just been promoted to being in charge of the junior

section of the library. Presumably this was because I've come up with loads of things for children over the past few years. Storytimes and drama sessions and children's book festivals and displays of children's drawings. Mrs. Lundmark, who had been in charge of the junior section up to now, would soon be retiring and wanted to cut down her hours. She still saw the traditional old school anthology as the norm for good children's literature, and seemed to have lost interest long ago; often we didn't set eyes on her: she tended to work down in the storeroom. She was more than happy for me to pep up her boring old section and left me to get on with it, although it wasn't really my job. And I did it because secretly I'm totally fascinated by children.

Yes, secretly! Because you can't admit it openly, you know, if you're a childless widow approaching thirty-five! If I'd as much as taken a kid on my knee, every female of my acquaintance—except Märta—would have delighted in pitying me, and I didn't want to give them the chance. And they'd have told themselves that at least they weren't childless, even if they were having counseling and/or were divorced and could only work part-time and were as poor as church mice. They complained that their kids kept them awake at nights and fought with their siblings and threw up in the car and refused to do their homework; they complained about the price of milk and soccer cleats and riding lessons. And then they had to go early because Pelle was running a temperature or Fia had a dental appointment. Or it was their turn in the town center parents' patrol, when they weren't dashing off to parents' evenings or taking their kids to violin lessons. "It's never a problem for you to do a bit of overtime," they said. "Aren't you lucky!"

So I fell into the habit of going back to work sometimes

in the evenings and putting in secret overtime! I got a real kick out of all those lively drawings, and I organized story-times just so I could stand there surreptitiously watching the children listen. Eyes on stalks, mouths half open, their bodies turned to the story like flowers to the sun.

I was a voyeur. Of children.

Embarrassing. Those of us who are childless aren't sup-posed to show any interest in children; it seems to provoke the Real Parents. "If only you knew," they sigh. "Sometimes I feel like hurling them against the wall."

Presumably they mean well.

I know, I know: the biological clock's ticking louder and louder! Märta hasn't any children, either, because her Passion is determined not to end up with any more; he's working hard on wriggling out of paying child support for the three he's already got, each with a different mother. She said once with a crooked smile that parents jolly well shouldn't be allowed to have children because they hadn't the sense to appreciate them.

Whereas we did. But then we never had to clear up the vomit in the car.

"Well, there's no way I could ever take a section head's job," Lilian said. "At home we have a catastrophe a week, at least, and no doubt that's how it'll be until my youngest's called up for military service. And you'll get a bit more on your salary. You might even get up to the same wage level as a new recruit in the parks department. And pay off your student loan before you die! Me, I can't even afford to join Weight Watchers—but it doesn't matter because I can't afford to buy food, either, ha ha! I expect it was Olof who recommended you . . ."

In one breath she succeeded in making it my fault that

her kids were starving and insinuating that I'd actually slept my way to the new job. Nice one, Lilian! No Sundays off for you from now on.

Biological clocks. I imagine them as big alarm clocks, with a little hammer oscillating wildly between two round bells to wake you up in a total panic, wanting only to go forth and multiply, or at least breed. I wonder if the biological clock also has a snooze function, so you can doze back off and be woken again a bit later? I'd be glad if it did.

Because just look at what the biological clock has done to me. Perverse reaction to the Forest Owner? And for all I know, he could have a whole bunch of kids, all with the same Forest Owner caps. I can imagine them all walking along in a row behind him, trowels in hand.

Tomorrow is my thirty-fifth birthday. No breakfast in bed for me, that's for sure. Because Märta's in Copenhagen with the Passion and Dad's never remembered a birthday, all that was Mum's business. And Mum—well, yes, she remembers birthdays past and present and is always jumping up to celebrate somebody's, even in the middle of the night, according to the staff on her ward. Though they never bear any relation to this year's calendar.

At work they'll be expecting me to treat them all to a slice of marzipan gateau, otherwise I won't get that bloody ceramic pot they've no doubt clubbed together to buy me at the posh handicraft shop.

Örjan used to give me birthday presents: tasteful, practical, and impersonal ones. A designer toaster and a bicycle helmet and once a pair of double-weave Norwegian long johns. But he never brought me breakfast in bed; he worked on the assumption we were both too nervous about spoiling our expensive down duvet.

40

The autumn plowing's out of the way and I'm not thinking of doing much in the forest this year, just a bit of trimming. This is the time when I should be getting down to repairing some of the machinery and recasting the concrete base for the manure and giving the tractor shed a coat of paint.

But I'm not.

The days go by; sometimes I come in from the cowshed and lie down on the settee and stare at the ceiling. Because if I stare out of the window, I only see all the things I haven't done. Sometimes I read the *Farmer*, and not just the news section: I read maniacally through all the small ads in the family section and all the death notices in the local paper. There's no point getting started on anything, it'll be time for milking again soon.

Five years ago there were still two of us farmers left in the village. Bengt-Göran had taken over from his dad, like me, and we'd sit over a beer in the evenings and plan to have joint grazing for the cows or build an outdoor milking shed in the pasture. But Bengt-Göran's brother-in-law, who's an economist and works for the local council, calculated it would be a totally loss-making venture. Then Bengt-Göran met Violet, and Violet liked going abroad on package holidays. Bengt-Göran had jealous visions of flashy cars down on the beach and mats of dark chest hair and gold crucifixes around necks, and before you could blink he'd sold the cows and started going on holiday with Violet. He went over to beef cattle and got someone from town who fancied escaping to the country to look after them whenever he was away. In winter he took on temporary snow clearance work. I don't see much of him any more.

Last autumn, before I knew Mum was ill, I used to take the car every evening and go out visiting people. Those that were still left in our village, I mean. The older ones gave me coffee and told me about their illnesses; the younger ones were always busy putting the kids to bed or repainting the kitchen cupboards. And every time they had a female cousin or some friend of their wife's staying, they'd invite me around on a Friday night to make up a foursome, and we'd have elk roast and a few glasses of wine and sometimes even dance. Sooner or later I'd find myself alone with the girl, and if I was drunk enough, we'd go and and find a place to be together, and that would be the end of it. This autumn I haven't been out in the car for an evening visit once, but people do come here occasionally. I'm a Good Neighbor, the neon sign on their foreheads flashes. Or perhaps I'm imagining things.

When I went into town to go to the bank the other day, I saw the beige woman again. She was going into the library, but she hadn't got any books with her as far as I could see. It occurred to me she might work there. And then . . . when I'd finished my business at the bank and came out into the street, I suddenly caught sight of my boots on their way through the glass doors of the library, with me in them! It was extraordinary.

In the light that was flooding through the glass roof above the desk, I started feeling nervous and turned my head to one side to sniff anxiously at the collar of my jacket and see if I smelled of the cowshed.

Then I caught sight of her. She was bending down to talk to a small child and pointing to something in a book. They were laughing.

I clumped over in my boots and tapped her on the shoulder. She straightened up with an irritated frown. When she saw it was me, she looked confused and a bit scared. And I was just as confused.

"Er—hello, by the way—have you got any books on beekeeping?" I blurted, trying not to smile my killer smile.

"I'm sure we have, and hello to you, too!" she said brusquely. "You can ask at the information desk. It's my lunch break at the moment."

The Prize Loser composed himself for a decisive pounce.

"Don't suppose you'd fancy . . . fancy . . . coming along to the cemetery with me?"

She gave me a long look.

"Hah, I bet that's what you ask all the girls!" she said, and then smiled like a child during summer holidays.

From that moment there are gaps in my memory, but I know nothing felt strange or awkward any longer.

She fetched her coat and off we went. I even thought her hairy wool hat looked nice. With its toadstools and everything.

We went somewhere to eat and I haven't a clue what we ate or said. Except one thing. When I wanted to pay for us both she said, "Well, yes, thank you. Because it's my thirty-fifth birthday today. And this can be my present."

That made me realize two things at once.

She wasn't expecting any other presents.

And I was in love with her.

There wasn't a sudden click or anything like that. It felt more like that time I accidentally leaned against the electric fence.

+✠+✠+✠+✠+✠+✠+✠+✠+✠+✠+✠+✠+✠+✠+✠+✠+✠+✠

My diary is full
of ownerless name days
and promises of full moons
ready for the taking

I was standing there in the library, talking to a cross little
girl who thought Snow White was stupid. "Fancy not recog-
nizing her own stepmother when she turned up with that
apple! Useless!" she said. We laughed.

Someone thumped me on the shoulder. It felt like the
long arm of the law, but it was the Forest Owner! He was
wearing his usual loud quilted jacket, but he'd taken off his
cap and his forehead was hidden by springy curls of dusty,
yellow hair. He looked angry, spitting out some unintel-
ligible reproach in a demanding tone. I assumed he was
complaining I hadn't tended the grave properly, and it took
me a few moments to realize he was looking for a book.

"Ask at the information desk, I'm at lunch!" I snapped.

His face twitched uncontrollably. Then he asked if I
fancied coming along to the cemetery with him.

The little girl was watching him with interest.

And suddenly I realized there was something I'd entirely misunderstood and lots more I didn't know at all.

So we went out and had lunch. He put away fantastic amounts of stew and beetroot and bread, and slurped a bit when he drank his milk, but I just sat there basking in the warmth of his smile. With his cap off and his face alive with attentiveness, he didn't look dreary, or well into middle age, just very real. And that hair was bewitching, there was no other word for it.

We chatted in a cheerful, random sort of way, and didn't say a word about Kristeva and Lacan—as far as I can recall we talked about Father Christmases, the various stages of casting concrete, yellow buntings, St. Peter's, and big toenails. He was so quick on the uptake it almost felt like telepathy.

I told him it was my birthday, and he seemed somehow to know I hadn't had any presents.

"You're coming with me!" he said, pulling on his cap and getting me into my coat in a decisive, manly way. Then he marched me off to the Domus department store and started buying birthday presents. He didn't ask me what I wanted, just told me to shut my eyes whenever he made up his mind about something. We visited all three floors and ended up in the coffee shop, where we ordered some cakes.

He spread all the carefully gift-wrapped parcels on the table and looked at me expectantly. I went at them with an eagerness that wasn't in the least faked, ripping them open one after another and exclaiming, "Ohhh!", "Wow!", and "You shouldn't have!"

On the ground floor he'd bought a pair of Mickey Mouse earrings; a butterfly-shaped soap; and some mauve tights. On the next floor, a shiny red ball; a poster with the silhouette of a loving couple hand in hand in a giant shell, sailing across the sea into the sunset; and a cap just as ghastly as the one he wears, but without the "Forest Owners' Alliance" logo.

In the last parcel there was a mouth organ.

"Can you play the mouth organ?" he asked.

I shook my head.

"Good! Me neither! I knew we must have something in common!" he beamed.

He was about to stab his fork into his third cake when his whole body stiffened. He'd caught sight of his watch.

"I've got to go," he cried. "I should have been back ages ago."

At that he leaped up, scattering paper and presents all over the place, and strode off to the escalator. Just as he was stepping onto it he turned around.

"What's your name?" he bellowed.

I felt a real fool shouting back "Desiréeeeeee!" Customers' jaws went dropping into their shopping carts all around.

"Whaaaat?" I heard from the escalator, but then he was gone.

"And you're Cinderella, I suppose," I muttered into my cake. "Better hold onto your boots!"

There was an odd atmosphere in the library staff room when I got back, three hours late and without any marzipan gateau.

It cost me dear. No, not the presents—but when I got to the cowshed an hour and a half late for milking, the cows were all bellowing at me. They'd eaten up all the feed and been lying in the shit and were so unsettled it took me several hours to deal with them. It was only when I switched on the washer afterward that I realized the milk from a cow that had just had penicillin had gone into the tank with all the rest, and that could only mean one thing: I'd have to throw away twenty-four-hours' worth of milk production, and quite apart from it costing me thousands of kronor I couldn't afford, I'd have to spend several more hours getting rid of the milk. But it was worth it. Definitely.

The only other time I did something as disastrous as that, I was fifteen. Mum worked as a home helper in those days, and I used to do the afternoon milking when I got in from school. We had a big end-of-year math exam coming up and I was worried about getting a good grade for my report and was brooding on some theorem. You mustn't do that. Farmers need to be as alert as fighter pilots every minute of the day, Dad used to say. Otherwise they find themselves under a speeding tractor or with a horn through their guts, or they slice their thigh with the power saw. We had to throw away seven hundred liters that time; Dad went and stuck his head in the water trough, but he didn't say much. I know he blamed himself all his life for me losing my fingers in the circular saw when I was four.

Not that my good grades in math did me much good. When Dad died, I left school and took over his job. Mum didn't want me to; she'd rather have given up the farm, she said, although it had been passed down through her family. I made up my mind one summer night when I saw her sitting under the big rowan in front of the house with her arm around the trunk, staring out over the grassy bank.

And I felt like one hell of a guy when my old classmates came around to see me and I screeched into the yard on the big tractor, jumped out in my steel-capped cowshed boots, and spat chewing snuff in all directions. We managed, with Granddad's help. And then he died and I had fewer and fewer visitors. I expect they got tired of me always being out working when they came, and even when they did get to see me, all I talked about was carcass weights and pulpwood prices. I understand how they felt.

Right, time to pull my socks up. Check which cows are in heat—I can't afford to miss any. Got to clean the harrow before it clogs up entirely. Ring the vet. And the bank, tomorrow. I'm behind with the bookkeeping. And almost out of wood.

Freezing cold in the house—I didn't have time to light the stove before I went to the cowshed. It'll be an hour before I can take a shower. First thing tomorrow I'll have to chop some more wood before I see to the cows. So I can take a shower after I've done the morning milking. Because I'm going into town to find her again and that's that. No, bugger it! Tomorrow I've got the inseminator and the vet coming, and I never know when to expect them. Damn!

I didn't have time to do any food shopping, either. What's left in that tin of herring I opened ages ago probably isn't fit for human consumption—and if I keeled over and died of botulism she'd never even know! Because she doesn't know my name! Would she wonder why I never got in touch again?

But I know her name, all right! Or at least, I sort of do. Holding a bit of soggy crispbread spread with almost rancid butter in one hand, I start looking up Wallin in the phone book.

There are eight of them, but none with girls' names. There's a D. Wallin with an address in Kofferdist Road—I couldn't make out what she was saying when she shouted her name. but it sounded like something beginning with "D." Only the Prize Loser of all Sweden would ring a person they don't know and ask to speak to "somebody beginning with D."

But I'll drive in on Friday, in time for lunch.

Aargh! Friday—I've got the test milking and the milk recorder's coming. Bugger!

I wake up the next morning on the settee in the sitting room with a half-eaten crispbread in my hand and a grin plastered across my face.

The knight has fallen from his horse
the totem poles are worm-eaten
and the steam engine must be constantly reinvented—
only the sunrise is the same as ever

When I got home, I kicked off my shoes and jumped up onto the sofa and pulled down a Käthe Kollwitz reproduction that used to be Örjan's pride and joy. It was a charcoal sketch of a tired-looking woman crying. Then I pinned up the poster of the couple in the seashell.

Next, I took off my dress and put on the Mickey Mouse earrings and the mauve tights and poured a glass of mulled wine (cold) and drank a toast to myself. It was the only alcohol I had in the house.

And I spent the whole evening in that outfit, trying to teach myself "Jingle Bells" on the mouth organ and letting my thoughts come and go. Finally I went out to the bathroom and took a long, hot bath, splashing around in the water with the red ball and stroking my skin with the butterfly soap.

I've had worse birthdays!

Then just as I'd dropped off to sleep, the phone rang. How did he get my number? was my first thought. But it was Märta, from Copenhagen. She wished me a happy birthday and said she was sorry she hadn't been able to ring earlier. Apparently she and Robert had been taken in for questioning by the police for some obscure reason; she couldn't go into details because she was still at the police station. I was answering her distractedly and eventually she noticed.

"So it's happened!" she said. Märta's senses are as keen as a foxhound's, at least where everybody except herself is concerned.

"I've met the boy next door. That's to say, the grave next door!" I giggled.

For once she was struck dumb. Then somebody barked something in Danish and the line went dead.

He didn't come to the library on Thursday. I dropped a tray of index cards and deleted an important computer file.

He didn't come on Friday, either. I took off the Mickey Mouse earrings at lunchtime. Lilian laughed at them and said they weren't really my style, if I didn't mind her saying. I laughed, too, and said they were a present from one of the storytime children.

It was almost true.

About three o'clock on Friday afternoon, Olof handed me a telephone receiver. "Somebody wanting to speak to 'a Miss Wallin'," he said. "I suppose that's you."

My stomach cramped as if I'd eaten something that disagreed with me. My fingers were slippery on the receiver.

"Yes, Desirée Wallin?"

"Desirée?" he said. He had a strong local accent, so it

sounded rather like "deyziray." But it was definitely him. I recognized the voice now.

"My name's Benny. Benny Söderström. I just took a chance on it being Wallin. From the gravestone."

"Yes."

"Can you meet me tomorrow? At the cemetery gate, about one?"

"Yes," I answered in another monosyllable. Quite the chatterbox.

It all went quiet.

"I can play 'Jingle Bells' now," I said.

"Bring the mouth organ with you then, and you can teach me!"

"Is that allowed, playing a mouth organ in the cemetery?"

"The residents don't tend to complain. And then we can go for something to eat. I haven't been able to get anything down for two days."

"Nor me."

"Good!" He rang off abruptly.

Olof was observing me closely. It must have been rather odd listening to my end of the conversation. Then he smiled sadly and patted me on the cheek. Life has made some impression on him, then. He recognizes a confused teenager when he sees one.

I knocked a box of disks onto the floor and sat down suddenly when I went to pick them up. And just couldn't stop laughing.

I couldn't find any clean socks and the pump stopped working, so there was no hot water, and when I came tearing along to the cemetery gates ten minutes late, I knew I stank of the cowshed. Sometimes, like when you go to the village shop, you forget you're wearing your overalls until you notice people moving out of range of the smell. They probably think it's a flatulence problem; not many people recognize ordinary cowshed smells these days.

She was wearing the mauve tights. They clashed with her coat.

"I smell of the cowshed, because I'm a farmer," I reeled off before I'd even said hello. "Twenty-four milk cows, plus followers." I hadn't even managed to tell her that, the time before.

". . . and a few sheep," I added. Sheepishly. And squinted at her as I tried to keep my distance and stay downwind.

She stared at me. Then her summer holiday smile spread slowly across her whole face. "What does followers mean?" she asked.

We decided a trip to the swimming pool was in order, and on the way I told her followers means young stock. I rented an awful pair of dark blue swimming trunks and bought a little sachet of shampoo and gave myself a good scrub, then we met at the edge of the pool. She'd wound her straight, white blond hair into a wet little sausage of a bun; I hardly recognized her.

Her swimsuit was beige, of course, and she was thin, you might almost say bony. If it hadn't been for her little plums of breasts you could easily have put her in the "male, 14–16" category. And yet—her slenderness was more greyhound than famine victim—her movements were sort of efficient and energy-saving; I watched spellbound as her pale hand painted pictures in the air as she spoke.

I thought how I'd always liked bright colors—and plenty of flesh and even rolls of fat for that matter, something to get a nice firm grip on. Decided I'd only ever use the very tips of my fingers if I ever got anywhere near her plums.

I once had a collie bitch I tried to mate with a dog of the same breed, a real pedigree animal. The bitch was climbing up the walls, frantic to get out—she totally refused to get it together with that particular dog. A few months later she stood there placidly letting herself be mounted by a Norwegian elkhound–Labrador cross.

There's no predicting how that sort of thing works.

We swam a few lengths and had a race on the exercise bikes, then we went to the cafeteria and made our choice from their selection of dry, crumbly almond cakes. We talked the whole time—well, mostly she did, of course.

In midsentence I felt her foot rubbing along my calf, and totally lost her drift. Children's shouts and screams echoing from the pool came together with the thumping in my ears, and I had to put my towel across my lap. We played footsie for a while and I struggled to keep my eyes on her face. All I could see was her mouth moving, but I've no idea what she was saying.

Suddenly she took hold of my damaged hand and started nibbling the fingerless knuckles. I sat stock-still.

"Let's go back to my place," she said.

So we did. To her white and beige apartment.

I shall remember it until the day I die.

She unlocked the door, threw her swimming things down in one corner and her coat in another. Then she turned to face me, peeled off her pale blue T-shirt and put her head to one side.

I peered furtively about me as I started pulling off my jeans. And then I went completely limp. It was like stripping off in the central library.

"All these bloody bookshelves are making me nervous!" I muttered.

"That's a new one!" she grinned, putting my empty knuckles to her lips again.

Then we made love, twice, straight off. No finesse—but it would have been as hard to stop as a high-speed train on a clear stretch of track.

The third time, I mumbled in her ear: "Now we're two dogs that'll be stuck fast in each other until someone throws a bucket of water over us!"

So then we started lurching around the apartment still joined together. She fried eggs and bacon with me inside her, behind her. She tied an apron around her front and my back.

We went for a shower like some eight-legged primeval creature.

We considered wrapping ourselves in a sheet and going down to buy an evening paper and scare the wits out of people, so we started practicing our footwork. But before we'd managed to get the sheet to fit properly, her eyes went out of focus and she sank down in a heap on the hall carpet. She kept saying something about red patches on her breasts; I never discovered what she was going on about.

For once I didn't have to look at my watch, because I'd talked Bengt-Göran into doing the evening milking, but there was still tomorrow morning to think of. I couldn't bear the idea of being parted from her even for a minute, so I asked her to come home with me.

The fourth time we slept together, I had time to feel her squeezing me inside her. She had muscles down there like a milkmaid's hands after a whole summer up in the mountain pastures. I told her so.

She rubbed her nose against mine.

"Do you think I can learn hand milking, too?" she murmured.

✦✠✦

Love makes others into doves,
gazelles, cats, peacocks—but I,
quivering, wet, and transparent—
am your jellyfish

Örjan and I used to read *The Joy of Sex* together. We'd massage one another with oil and then try all the positions, even a strange pretzel-shaped one. I often faked orgasms. Not to make Örjan happy, I have to admit—I just couldn't go on sometimes, and he never liked to give up until he'd achieved the goal he'd set himself. It was the same with his research, actually—he'd put forward a hypothesis and not give up until he'd proved it.

But he'd certainly read somewhere that women get red blotches on their breasts after orgasm, and when I stayed my usual white, he'd get an irritated frown and look as if he was going to start all over again. I tried taking the line that I was short of pigment, but that made him launch into an account of the difference between pigmentation and nerve stimulation, until I fell asleep from exhaustion.

I'd assumed I just wasn't naturally erotically inclined.

I was wrong.

When I came out of the ladies' changing room at the pool and scanned the bathers through squinting eyes, I couldn't at first identify my Forest Owner. I was looking out for a lumbering walk and that blessed cap with the earflaps. And there he suddenly was beside me, in rented swimming trunks, narrow-hipped and broad-shouldered, his arms wiry, with veins like twisted rope. Face and lower arms tanned, the rest of his body white as chalk. That dusty yellow hair had gone into wet golden-brown curls.

When I stroked his calf with my big toe in the cafeteria, he put his towel across his lap with an embarrassed grin. I didn't miss that. My ovaries turned somersaults and I couldn't get him back home quick enough.

Of course, it was still Desirée Wallin who spent that afternoon at her home address with a man. I mean, I had the same personal identity number and driver's license and birthmarks as I'd had that morning. And yet I wasn't the same person. Maybe it was a sudden case of split personality, the sort you read about in the Sunday supplements.

He hadn't just turned my head, he'd rotated it so many times that it came off and I had to hold it on a string like a balloon, while my body twisted and wallowed. Hour after hour. I even found time to spare a thought for Örjan when those red patches flared.

Reading in a book about all those different lovemaking techniques can sometimes make me yawn. The concept's always the same. But when they're happening to you, it's like a nine on the Richter scale. I only have to think about it to feel giddy all over again.

Toward evening we were red and puffy and getting sore in several places. He informed me I was coming home with him, and I threw my toothbrush and shampoo into a bag.

No nightie. But I put on the cap he gave me for my birthday. He had a hulking great car, half truck, and I had to shift half a ton of scrap iron before I could squeeze in beside him. We stopped at a gas station on the way and bought a chunk of cheese and a baguette. He gestured vaguely toward the condoms; I shook my head and drew a coil in the condensation on the window. It was still in place, as a reminder of Örjan.

It was dark when we reached his farm, so I couldn't get any real idea of my surroundings. But it smelled reassuringly rural and the house was a big, old wooden one, painted red. He ushered me through the porch and into the hall, then disappeared toward the cowshed to do one last evening check.

There was a faintly rural smell even indoors, not very pleasant, to tell the truth. Mildew and sour milk and wet dog.

So I was on my own for my first meeting with his house, which was definitely a pity—I could have done with his warm, dry left hand and its three remaining fingers. Because there was no mistaking that this was where the man with the tasteless gravestone lived.

I started in the kitchen. There was a fluorescent strip light on the ceiling with a few dead flies in it. The walls were grayish blue and clearly had been for the last fifty years. They were fly-specked in some places, in others hung with cross-stitch samplers, some with sayings like "In this Home we find our Rest when Clean and Tidy have done their Best," and pictures of bright orange flowers in brown baskets, kittens, bluetits, and red cottages. On the windowsill stood a row of potted plants as dead as the dusty everlasting flowers in the vintage black fifties-design vase. There was a kitchen stool with a grubby rag rug on the seat, a dirty tea towel, rib-backed wooden chairs with seat cushions in a brown floral fabric. Perched on top of the refrigerator, which was so old it was freestanding and had rounded corners, were a blue fabric flower in a china shoe and a plastic cat, virtually transparent with age. I put the cheese in the refrigerator; it was all but empty and smelled of compost.

I felt my way into the next room. There was a big black switch by the door, at hip height; dark green embossed vinyl wallpaper, the sort that makes it look as if there's moss growing on the walls; an old couch with one end kicked through, covered in an odd assortment of shabby rugs; an oak sideboard with a large television set standing on it, an oval mirror hanging above it; an angular, fifties-style armchair; a magazine rack full of old copies of the *Farmer,* and more cross-stitch pictures. Plus a framed reproduction of "Urchins at the Farm Gate."

I gaily told myself: you could open a postmodernist cult café in here! The thought went through my mind that if I'd come across a place like this in Estonia, say, I might have found it touching, even exotic. But I could feel the corners of my mouth trembling with the effort of holding that smile.

And they drooped definitively when I got to the bedroom and saw the unmade bed with the gray-looking sheets.

I went in through the cellar door and used the downstairs shower so I didn't spread the cowshed smell around the house. I've tried to avoid using it much recently, because to be honest, it needs a good scrub. I'll need the pressure hose if I'm ever going to get it clean again. And there are various other places in the house that could do with it, too. But how the hell to find time?

Mum used to work at least a ten-hour day, and I must work fifteen; that would make twenty-five, which I couldn't count up to even if I used toes as well as fingers. Let's face it: sparkling tiles are as much a thing of the past as homemade buns and crisply pressed sheets.

As I stood humming to myself in the shower, I thought I could picture her, my beige beloved, moving her small, pale hands over the kitchen table, laying out that delicious home-cured salt beef we always used to have, and a loaf of sweet, dark bread, and a cold beer. And wafer rolls coated in pearl sugar.

She wasn't, of course. Where would she have got wafer rolls from, just like that? She hadn't even unpacked the shopping or put the water on for tea. She was standing there in front of the bookcase in the sitting room, arms dangling at her sides, staring at the spines of the books. She didn't find any lost treasures there, I'm afraid. My old school books and a few things from Mum's reading circle— and fifteen years' worth of ancient bound volumes of the *National Farming Magazine*.

I didn't feel very comfortable. Despite getting so carried away at her apartment, I had noticed she'd got two walls covered in books.

"Looking for some bedtime reading? Would you like *Elementary School Chemistry* or the *National Farming Magazines* for 1956? Thrilling year for pig breeding, that one," I ventured. She gave me a tired smile. Not a summer holiday smile, not at all.

We went out to the kitchen and I started noisily getting cups out and putting water on to boil. She sat down at the table and began leafing through the agricultural supplies catalogue.

It felt a bit strange. I mean, the fact that she expected to be waited on like that.

"I've been all through higher education," she said suddenly, "and I can always answer the current affairs quiz in the newspaper without cheating. But even so, I had no idea there were any such things as self-loading trailers or bras for cows."

I said nothing. She was trying to make a point. I put

the bread on the table and she reached for it absentmind-
edly.

"I mean, I expect you deal with those sorts of things
every day and know them back to front. They're no
stranger for you than Lacan's theories are for me."

"Who?" I said. "Lackong?" He was some bloke at Alfa
Laval, wasn't he? Invented the milk separator?

Of course I realized that she meant it kindly. That I
shouldn't feel I was, like, stupid because I hadn't got any
books and hadn't been to college, and that she was ignorant
in her own way, blah, blah, blah. It riled me, even so. Who
the hell did she think she was, coming here and consoling
me for not being her? I must have sounded sulky, because
she peered at me through her fringe.

"I just mean that sitting here on the settee there should
be a girl with thick blond plaits saying, 'Benny, have you
seen, they've got some new styles of cow bra this year! And
don't you think you should invest in a Krone 2400 self-
loader?' I don't know the first thing about what you do."

"If it was a girl like that I was looking for, I'd have
applied to the farmers' relief service," I said. "Or put a
personal ad in the *Farmer*. 'WLTM woman with tractor
license, appearance no object, unpaid.' But if you pick up
girls in cemeteries, you have to make do with what you get.
And anyway, weren't you going to learn hand milking?"

That brought out the summer holiday smile.

"Have you got anything I can practice on?" she said.

I had. There and then.

We dragged ourselves to bed; I didn't even manage to
change the sheets, though I'd certainly planned to.

I was woken in the middle of the night by her sitting up
in bed, her breath coming fast and panicky.

64

"Örjan?" she said in a dry little voice, feeling my arm with sweaty fingers.

"You're with me now," I mumbled, stroking her arm until she calmed down. She took my three fingers and laid them over her mouth and went back to sleep with a sigh.

✦✖✦✖✦✖✦✖✦✖✦✖✦✖✦✖✦✖✦✖✦✖✦✖✦✖

Good running shoes and a reliable compass—
what help are they
if I don't know
which way up the map goes?

I was woken by Benny, sitting on the side of the bed, trying to plait my thin, straight hair.

It felt like the middle of the night, and there was a nightmare lurking dimly at the back of my mind. Something about Örjan trying to get me into a life jacket. "But I'm only going in a shell," I tried to say, but when I looked around me I couldn't see land in any direction. I moaned.

Benny threw himself across me to the far side of the bed and started plaiting my hair that side. "We should be able to get you looking the part," he said. "Though you did sleep through the morning milking." His hair was wet and he smelled of soap.

"Get lost, country bumpkin," I croaked. "Take your cows and go! Bring me a café au lait in bed, with croissants and the review section of the paper! Then you can go and listen to the farming news or something!"

He twisted the plaits into place on top of my head

and fastened them with a rubber band the size of a bicycle tire. "That's how you ought to look for work in the cowshed tomorrow," he said. "And wear wellies and waddle along with your hips swaying, lecturing them on hoofcare."

I did the waddling part all right. I was all swollen between the legs.

"See what happens if you don't watch out for untethered bulls," he said with satisfaction.

We went down to the kitchen and I carried on chewing my way through the boring gas-station bread. Benny shoveled down porridge with applesauce as if he had hollow legs. He asked if I made my own bread, and I said I thought bread grew on trees, and you either picked it as little rolls or let it ripen into big, fat loaves.

He laughed, but it sounded a bit forced.

Then he dragged me out to view the property, impatient to show me everything. I nodded and said aha and oh ho and ooh yes, kind sir. It wasn't difficult, because the farm was in a beautiful setting: in a landscape of rolling hills, with the last golden leaves of autumn to complete the pretty picture. Light trails of mist across rich, black soil he'd just plowed for winter. Gleaming rowanberries, the sort his mother used to make a delicious jelly with, he told me . . . Enormous plastic bags full of some kind of soured grass in neat rows behind the barn. And finally, a cowshed full of well-fed, sleepy cows—I've rarely seen a life-sized cow in the flesh; they seemed almost unreal.

Of course, I made straight for the calf pens and let the doe-eyed little creatures suck my fingers, but Benny dragged me away to show me the finer points of his new manure-handling system. He can't really have believed I was the slightest bit interested? The sheep were still outside, "but we'll have to get them in soon!" he said. We?

I had a sense of being in the middle of someone else's dream. Someone was about to land herself an attractive farm owner with twenty-four dairy cows. Plus followers. Though really, someone hadn't asked for anything like that at all, but had got quite used to the idea of being an old maid, perhaps with a cat. And lovers in small doses to keep her hormones in balance.

It was, like, too much, as Märta would put it. Yes, too much by at least twenty-four. But I didn't say it. He was so proud.

Then, of course, there was a big fuss when I decided I wanted to go home. I'd had just about as much cross-stitch embroidery and manure-handling gadgetry as I could take for one day. I needed to pamper my battered undercarriage in a hot bath and read the newspaper and listen to a bit of Boccherini and lie on clean white sheets and drink herbal tea.

I needed to think.

But before I'd had time to put any of that into acceptable words, Benny threw me a kilo of frozen ground beef straight from the freezer and said eagerly that it would be fine for our dinner—maybe meatballs? I stared from him to the ice-cold lump and back again. Then I said something labored about still being in culture shock and needing to be put back in my natural habitat for a while.

He looked at me, and I had an almost tangible sense of his long antennae moving over my face. Yes, he's sensitive to emotional moods. I suppose you have to be if you need to make contact with our dumb friends the animals.

And his wonderful smile clouded over.

"Sure. I'll give you a lift," was all he said. "There are no buses from here on Sundays."

So he drove me the forty kilometers to town, ran his hand lightly over my hairy wool hat, and dropped me off in the street. Because he was in a hurry to get back for evening milking.

When I unlocked the door and looked about me in the flat, which we'd left in such a state the day before, my mood changed again, and I rushed back out onto the landing. Should I have accepted the challenge of the frozen lump, just so I didn't have to see his smile snuffed out?

Though there was no way I could have turned it into meatballs, even so; and that was probably the sticking point. Örjan and I ate vegetarian meals, and since he died, the only meatballs in my kitchen have been the frozen, pre-packaged sort. I haven't stood eye to eye with a homemade meatball since I lived at home with Mummy. And she wasn't one to let her little Desirée soil her scholarly hands with messy ground meat.

She wouldn't be able to teach me how to make them now, even if I asked her to. The last time I went to visit her, she called me Sister Karin and told me off because no one had brought her coffee.

I turned again, went back into the apartment, and started running the bathwater.

It wasn't that I didn't notice something wasn't right. She was about as excited by what I showed her on the farm as she would've been if I'd given her a detailed account of my digestive system. Polite, yes. Asked quick-witted questions. But not what you'd call starry-eyed with interest.

I kept telling myself I'd have been just the same if she'd tried taking me around the library explaining what the letters on the shelves meant and how they organize the card indexes. But I didn't really convince myself. I mean, books are still just books. A farm is a farm.

And when I gave her a pack of frozen ground beef, I knew from the moment I lobbed it in her direction, while it was still in midair, that it was the Wrong Thing.

I hadn't really thought it through; I live in the sort of place where the men bring a dead elk home to the women and later sit down to an appetizing elk stew without ever wondering about the stages in between. I suppose my thoughts went roughly along the lines of: I'll have time to see to the calves while she gets us some dinner, then there'll be time to eat and have an after-dinner nap—ha ha— before evening milking. She looked at the meat as if it were a frozen cow pie. And then she wanted to go home. There was nothing I could do.

She sat with her hand on the back of my neck all the way home in the car. Now and then her fingers played with my hair.

"I didn't mean to offend you," the fingers said. "And don't go thinking it's all over between us!"

But no one else in the car was saying anything.

That evening I went over to Bengt-Göran and Violet's.

"We saw you had a girl with you!" said Violet, clearly curious.

Bengt-Göran gave me a wink and nudged me in the side, smiling the way he might have done if we'd just watched a porn film together. Well, we used to do that sort of thing occasionally, before Violet.

"Someone from town, eh?" he said eagerly.

Bengt-Göran kind of thinks girls from town are permanently in heat, and wear sexy black lace panties with slits in the crotch, and lie back and part their legs the minute you get them alone. That's comical, considering what a meek little town it actually is. And considering the way I once got laid in the hay by Bengt-Göran's own sister, who held me tight by the scruff of the neck. I was fourteen and she was seventeen; it was my first time—and my last, with her at any rate. I was petrified and went out of my way to avoid her after that. She didn't have lace panties; in fact, she didn't have any at all. Bengt-Göran doesn't know anything about it, of course. His sister's got four kids now, and looks like a sumo wrestler.

"Mmmm. A girl from town. I found her in the cemetery. I mean, that's where we happened to meet."

"Yeah, she did look a bit pale . . ." Bengt-Göran began with a snigger, but Violet just looked disapproving.

"The cemetery?" she said. "You always did like to be different, didn't you, Benny?"

I don't know what I've done to deserve Violet thinking I'm so odd. Maybe it was that time at a party when she and I were sitting talking, confiding in each other like you do when you've had a few. I told her I thought she'd be just the person to help Bengt-Göran cope with his archetypal farmer's melancholy. Farmer's melancholy! It makes me squirm with embarrassment to think of it now.

"Just look at him, sitting there so quiet and introspective in all this din," I hiccuped. "He's just drunk," Violet snapped. And she was right, of course; he threw up in a lilac bush straight after.

"She can't even make meatballs," I said. "All she can do is read books and talk about Lackong and his theories."

Best lay it on with a trowel. Don't want them expecting to be invited around for coffee and wafer rolls and engagement announcements in a hurry. Things are tricky enough as it is.

"Can't make *meatballs*!" said Violet, eyeing the table with great satisfaction. On it stood a serving dish the size of a washtub, brimming with crisp brown meatballs. "Would you like some, by the way?"

"That's right, Benny!" laughed Bengt-Göran, and his

porn film look was back. "She's disposable. Don't get bogged down in any marriage plans."

In Bengt-Göran's world there's no way you could get really fond of a woman who can't make meatballs, still less marry her.

As Violet handed me a heaped plateful, with lingonberry sauce made from berries she'd picked herself, I was on the verge of agreeing with him.

Trying the taste of loneliness,
letting a silent minute melt on my tongue,
only the dusty sunbeam intrudes

My apartment looks out on a garden surrounded on all sides by three-story blocks. All these apartments must be about twenty years old; the trees are tall and mature—we can see them through our windows. The sandpits are often deserted; the children who used to spend their time digging there, fifteen years ago, have flown the nest, but their middle-aged parents still live here. Splendid, dull people with no objectionable habits.

So it's very quiet outside my windows. They face south, and the sun finds its way in through my wooden-slatted blinds, making stripes on my white sofas. Occasionally I hear footsteps on the stairs outside, but not often; I live on the top floor. If I open the window, there's a rustling in the potted fig plant, the one Örjan grew. But I'm always too chilled to the bone to have it open for long; instead I have all the radiators permanently on high, and the temperature in here's usually at least seventy-three degrees.

I like lying on one of the sofas in my white dressing gown, watching the sun's rays stripe the air of the room.

Sometimes I raise a hand and let the sun make stripes on that, too, and the only sounds are the hum of the refrigerator and a late autumn fly blundering against the window, heavy thuds in the silence.

Of course I know this thing with Benny is impossible.

Like sitting in the shade of the plane tree on the last day of the holiday, drinking cold retsina and dreaming of uprooting yourself and just moving down there and taking each day as it comes. Getting some sort of job, finding a whitewashed house of your own, with a sun terrace covered in pots of herbs. And all the time you know that in five hours you'll be standing at Stockholm airport in the drizzle, and the next day you'll be sitting there at your desk in your ergonomic chair getting stressy, and the only thing left will be your suntan. And even that'll get washed down the drain in the bath before two weeks are out.

That was the way I dreamed as I thought of Benny and our games—there must be a way of hanging on to it all! Lock the front door and keep him in the wardrobe until I get home from work. Like in that cult film, the Spanish one with Antonio Banderas.

I tried imagining myself into his life. But no images came.

I hadn't been prepared for quite such a culture shock, in the home of a Swedish man of about my own age, living just forty kilometers away.

I'd probably have found it easier to adapt to a devout Muslim.

I immediately visualized a tall, thin man with sad eyes,

forced into political exile and living in a one-roomed council apartment with the walls covered in reams of Persian poetry. He worked day shifts as a cleaner, despite his university education back home, and at nights sat in smoky venues with his political and poetic friends, or went to see unforgettable black-and-white films at obscure little cinemas. And I'd find out about his culture and translate his poems and collect money on the streets for his campaign against the dictatorship. We'd sit on beautiful rugs eating spicy dishes.

But making meatballs in Benny's disgusting kitchen, and being a slave to twenty-four cows every day of the week, all year round? Keeping his discolored shower clean, stoking the stove with firewood whenever I needed hot water, discussing articles in the *Farmer*? Me?

I may be a racist, but I'm not the ordinary kind.

Even so, I clung to the phone obsessively for several days. Sometimes because it never rang, sometimes because I never rang.

To dispel that humiliating teenage feeling, I spent the evenings out. Worked overtime, went to the cinema, or on pub crawls with unmarried colleagues. They found me unusually happy and sociable, and so did I.

The weather got worse as autumn wore on; I hadn't even got the sunbeams to play with any longer. And in the dirty gray daylight, my apartment was about as inspiring as a dentist's waiting room. The only thing that broke the monotony was the neon-colored sunrise behind the loving couple in the shell, on the poster Benny had given me for my birthday.

Not an hour passed without my thinking of Benny.

At the library I started getting engrossed in the *Farmer*, to Lilian's unfettered delight. I said I was looking for an article the local authority had requested. About unblocking drains.

Olof sometimes looked at me as if he might be going to ask me something. But wisely, he never did.

One day I took it into my head to go for lunch to a café frequented by immigrants, men from various other countries. I stared at them so fixedly and thoughtfully from my lonely table that they completely misinterpreted my intentions and I ended up in awkward exchanges that I'd really rather forget. Especially as my reason for being there was so confused—not to say stupid—that I blushed all over.

As the days passed, my old depression came back, as good as new. And Märta still hadn't come home. I took baths that lasted half the night, until my skin was white and wrinkled, and dragged home bagloads of cheap paperback fantasy fiction. I wore down the butterfly soap until it was no more than a shapeless pink blob.

How could something that had felt so right turn out so wrong?

And Benny was by now presumably asking himself the same question. Since he didn't get in touch.

Every time I picked up the receiver to dial her number, I just sat there until I was cut off by the tone. She said she'd had a culture shock and needed to be alone. So I waited three days for her to ring. Then I rang. No answer.

I found an old "get well soon" card, put her address on it, stuck a stamp on, and tore it up.

Several times I thought of driving into town and going to the library. But I decided that would be too extreme.

The weather got worse and worse. It took me two days to get the sheep in, with the help of my neighbor's thirteen-year-old lad. They'd been outside for far too long and had muscles like elite gymnasts. The young rams went sailing over the fences with room to spare and the ewes were leaping about like deer. If I sent them to the abattoir now, they'd bring me in about as much as I could spend on a single blow-out at McDonalds. If I slaughtered them at home with old Nilsson to help me, we'd hardly be able to saw through the accumulations of muscle. The lad and I ran to-and-fro in the sleet, swearing like troopers. Well, mostly he did. "Fuck you!" he shrieked at the sheep.

I don't know why I hang onto them. It was Mum's idea to have a few; she used to use the wool for her knotwork classes. And she used to make a lamb stew with potatoes and beans that was hard to beat. It never occurred to me to learn how to cook it.

It wouldn't feel right to get rid of her sheep. One of the hardest things I've ever done was going through her room, just after she died. Throwing out clothes that still smelled of Mum, handling her reading glasses and medicines and knitting patterns. Nothing had prepared me for the fact that this would need doing. So I took the easy way out, of course: put the whole lot in a couple of old suitcases and took it up to the attic. And I haven't done anything with her room except take the sheets off the bed. She had the whole windowsill full of those plants with little bluey-mauve flowers. Expect they're all dead by now.

What the hell did she mean when she said culture shock?

This morning I was in town. There were a few things I needed to do. More than once, I thought I caught sight of her. At the agricultural supplier's, at Berggren's ironmonger's, at the dairy!

Bengt-Göran's dropped by two evenings in a row, no doubt to check out my sinful woman from town in close quarters.

"I'm not sure I'll be bringing her here again," I told him. He gasped in dumb admiration. Let him think I just dispose of women whenever it suits me.

He doesn't need to know that I'm longing for her, or that I take the phone upstairs and plug it in beside my bed at nights.

✠✖✖✖✠✖✠✖✠✖✖✠✖✠✖✠✖✠✖✠✖✠✖✠✖✠✖✠✖✠✖✖✠✖✠✖✠✖✖

Dismay seized all the Cherubs now;
to God there flew a horde—
"What Salami and Zulamith have built,
now see, O Lord!"

[From "The Milky Way" by Zacharias Topelius]

Märta finally came home from Copenhagen. She was waiting for me after work with a shopping bag in which she'd
got some Danish beer and a souvenir, a plastic snowstorm
with a naked couple inside. We went back to my place and
made tea and stretched out on the sofas.

She gave me an evasive answer when I asked what they'd
really been up to in Copenhagen.

"We're not here to talk about me!" she said. "You know
that very well!"

So I gave her a totally uncensored account of the last
week. With Märta there's no point wasting your effort trying anything else; she still manages to fish up most of it
from your muddy depths.

I spared her none of the details. The tasteless gravestone,

the dorky cap, the embroidery, the fly specks, and the mossy wallpaper. She snorted.

"I don't know what you think you're doing," she said. "That man sounds the ideal playmate for you! And you sit here worrying about home furnishings! Why should his cross-stitch bother you? After all, I don't suppose he embroidered it himself; he just didn't want to get rid of things that remind him of his parents. Have you really been going around imagining all Swedish farmhouses look like Carl Larsson paintings inside?"

That brought me up short. If I'd had any mental image at all of the inside of a Swedish farmhouse, it probably had been something along Carl Larsson lines. A big kitchen with an open fire burning in the grate, copper pans, and ring loaves hung on a pole along the ceiling. She'd touched a raw nerve there, so I raised my voice.

"You know as well as I do it's not a question of home furnishings! This is about two lifestyles on a total collision course! I'm never letting any cross-stitch over my threshold, and I don't suppose he'd let a Käthe Kollwitz over his—let's face it, this isn't just a matter of taste!"

"So why did you put up the poster with the couple in the seashell?" she asked slyly.

"Because he made me feel so happy . . ." I mumbled.

She gave a knowing nod.

"But you can't honestly imagine *me* on a three-legged stool with a milk pail jammed between my knees?"

"You weren't there for a bloody job interview!" Märta roared. "That guy gave you the best lay you've had for decades, maybe ever. And you've had a good laugh with him, which is more than you ever did with that bird fanatic you were married to! So what do a few fly specks matter? Don't be such a bloody coward! Grab it while you can! Otherwise you might just as well go in there and pull your pristine duvet cover over your head."

"But what should I do? I don't know what he's thinking! He hasn't been in touch!"

Märta held up the snowstorm with the pair of lovers inside.

"What you do is take this and a couple of Danish beers, right, and buy a pack of frozen meatballs, and go out there and surprise him tomorrow night. He made the first move; take it in turns and you might get somewhere! You can borrow my car."

A picture came into my mind of Salami and Zulamith. They're two characters in "The Milky Way," an old poem by Zacharias Topelius that I fell in love with when I was little, though I hardly understood a word of it. With Mummy's help I learned it by heart, and at her coffee parties she used to stand me proudly on the table and get me to recite it for her bored guests.

Salami and Zulamith are a man and a woman who each live on separate stars and love each other so much that they build a bridge of stars through space. I had a sudden vision of us taking it in turns: competent bricklayer Benny, trowel in hand, fixing star to star at his end, while I at mine tried to jump between the stars as if they were ice floes . . .

Märta's advice isn't always foolproof, but it usually involves some action that moves things forward. The following evening, I packed a basket with Danish beer, frozen meatballs, ready-made potato salad, and a (shop-bought) blueberry pie. And Märta's snowstorm with the lovers, wrapped up in gold paper. Then I drove out to Benny's farm. There was no answer to my knock, but the door was unlocked and the kitchen light was on, so I went in.

The strip light was buzzing, and a black monster of a radio on the draining board was blaring out some commercial station. I switched over to the shipping forecast and started bustling about; soon the air inside the grubby bobble-trimmed curtains was thick with a comfortable, childhood sort of feeling. I cleared a dirty porridge bowl off the table and put it to soak in cold water in the sink, along with the one already floating there. Then I searched drawers and cupboards until I came across china and cutlery, found a dainty embroidered tablecloth in the oak sideboard in the sitting room, and fried meatballs in a less than hygienic frying pan. When I heard him clomping up the stairs from the cellar, I had a sense of déjà vu: this had happened before.

"What the hell . . ." He stopped in the doorway, dressed in his cowshed gear. Then he strode across to me, molting straw and chaff, and gave me a mighty hug.

"Oh, meatballs?" he grinned. "Did you fry them all by yourself, my pale little lady?"

"Don't go thinking I shall make a habit of it!" I mumbled into his rank-smelling orange Helly Hansen jacket.

It was the best thing she could possibly have done—though I still feel I've got meatballs coming out of my ears. Violet had given me a bucketload to bring home; I'd been living off them for three days.

Shrimp spent the night with me, and as I was changing the sheets, she said she'd got her period and hoped she wouldn't leak on them.

Be my guest, I thought, because I liked the fact that she was saying it. It felt so intimate, homely even. You don't bother going to visit a short-term lover if your period's just started. She was sort of elevating me to more permanent status; no rush for the lovemaking. That wasn't what she'd come for.

Actually, I'd quite like a stain left by her on my sheets. There's probably a Latin name for perversions like that.

We lay talking for hours. And we were so happy the

whole time; we couldn't stop prattling. I remember that particularly.

"I'll give you culture shock!" I said. "I'll get myself a traditional costume! Yellow breeches and a double-breasted jacket with silver buckles. And you'll have to weave the cloth for my waistcoat, and then, you know what? Then I'll strut about outside the church on Sundays with my thumbs stuck in my waistcoat, discussing the weather and the harvest with the other farmers, and everybody'll know me as Big Benny of Rowan Farm! And you'll have to hold your tongue and make coffee for the entire congregation!"

"So I suppose a hundred years ago you'd have been quite a solid and prosperous farmer? With twenty-four cows?"

"You bet I would! And a lay magistrate and church-warden into the bargain. A well-to-do farmer with loads of farmhands to boss about, and pretty farm girls whose bottoms I could pinch. The villagers would have wanted Big Benny's opinion on everything, and invited me to join the parish council. Instead of which, here I am running around on my own from machine to machine like a headless chicken, and haven't even got time to go to union meetings."

"Would you have asked for the hand of the slender maiden from the town with nothing but a chest of books to her name?"

"Of course not! Benny of Rowan Farm's got to marry fat Brita from the farm next door, to extend his property. But I'd have hired the slender little thing as a maid and crept down to her on the kitchen settle at nights and got her pregnant. And I'd have paid decently for all her children and taken them on as shepherd boys and shepherdesses, whatever fat Brita had to say about it."

"But one day the slender maid runs away with Emil, the gypsy with the fiddle! What does Benny do then?"

"Then he kicks out her kids, too, and hires a new maid for the kitchen! A younger one!"

She clipped me on the ear with the pillow and we tussled for a bit. Then I had to give in, or I'd have needed to go for a cold shower.

Her panting subsided.

"I'm never going to be a kitchen maid, you know that, don't you?" she said. "And I wouldn't be worth having, anyway. I don't know how to bake or do washing or deal with all the bits from a slaughter. Isn't the farmer's woman supposed to cut the pig's throat and drain off the steaming blood and make it into some disgusting kind of dish?"

"Dunno. We've got an arrangement to have our meat back from the abattoir. Jointed and everything."

It all went quiet.

"But that bit about creeping down to me on the kitchen settle and getting me pregnant . . ." she said, as if to herself. "Hearing stuff like that turns me to jelly down there. The biological clock's ticking like mad."

I turned on my stomach and whimpered.

"You mustn't say things like that. These sheets'll be pregnant with little pillowcases before I can stop myself!"

She fell asleep with my knuckles pressed to her lips, again.

I ring home:
unobtainable.
"This—number—has—no—subscriber!"
Not even the answering machine can give me an answer.

So we embarked on the painstaking process of getting to know each other.

It was anything but straightforward, despite the fact that we outwardly seemed such free agents.

We were both without parents—he, definitively, I in practice. Mummy's been in a care home for five years now, and rarely recognizes me. Daddy just seems to think I'm disturbing him when I do occasionally go home to see him, especially if I try to talk to him.

He was like that even when I was little, actually. He disliked the slightest mention of what he called "women's matters": home and children, cooking, clothes, decor, and, of course, anything that could come under the heading of "feelings." Among women's matters he also included art, literature, and religion. . . . Above all, he hated any complaint relating to the female body. Not a word was to be breathed of these in his hearing; it was as if he was afraid of catching girl germs. As soon as he decently could, he disappeared off to the regiment. He was a major.

I sometimes wonder if he's really a homosexual. It's an odd thought, but then I've never been very close to my father. I mean, it's classic for children to shiver with amazement at the thought that their parents have done "it"; they count their siblings and think, "They must have done it at least three times." In my case there's good reason to suspect he only ever did "it" once, at least with Mummy. I've decided not to think about it, just to be glad it did happen that one time, at least.

So Mummy had nothing else to do except look after me. I was the doll with the shutting eyes that was finally hers, and she loved me as fervently as you do when you've been yearning for something too long. The long wait didn't exactly leave her critical or clear-sighted, either.

She came from a wealthy home. Grandfather had a canning factory that did brilliantly during the war—if I know anything about the old man, he probably made his fortune out of foxes and squirrels labeled and sold as "game." Daddy came from a Good Family, and once I heard the ladies in Mummy's bridge group whispering that he'd married Mummy because of his huge gambling debts. Sounds anachronistic but could very well be true; there's a straight line of descent from those types who shot themselves outside the casino in Monte Carlo at the turn of the last century to the sort who can't drag themselves away from the one-armed bandits in today's arcades. It's asking for trouble to ring Daddy while the lottery drawing is on.

When I was a child, Mummy had dyed, brassy yellow hair that she set in stiff curls with Carmen Curlers. She was nearly forty when she got married, and forty-two when I was born, and she'd never needed to earn her living. It was her idea to christen me Desirée, the much-desired daughter, and it was a beautiful thought, but I came to hate that name when I was at school, where I was bullied off and on, and they called me Dizzy.

I wanted to be called Kitty. Or Pamela.

Maybe being bullied is the fate that awaits any child who's been brought up to consider themselves the eighth wonder of the world, and doesn't encounter grim reality until they get to school.

Anyway, my parents' marriage was utterly invisible. They somehow contrived to live together, but totally independently of each other, in a large apartment with oak parquet and rows of interconnecting rooms, where Mummy had chosen the furniture and Daddy hung his peaked cap. They never argued in my presence, and most probably never in my absence, either. Daddy generally ate in the mess; Mummy and I would spend my summer holidays on our own, staying at a succession of guest houses. Daddy was always "on maneuvers."

At home, we didn't have a social life or any parties worthy of the name—there were occasional visits from bridge-playing ladies and their husbands, or Daddy's colleagues and their wives, for dreary three-course dinners with hired serving help. Madeira in cut glass, and cigarillos in special tins for offering around. I would be allowed to come in and say hello, my bony legs and arms protruding from the velvet dresses purchased for the occasion. Red-faced men would thump me on the back until I coughed, and say the girl needed to get out in the fresh air more and get some color in her cheeks. Mummy would have more curls than usual.

I never saw Mummy and Daddy touch each other, not even walk arm in arm.

So how was I to know what a marriage should look like? No wonder I thought Örjan and I had a model relationship. And it was hardly surprising I wasn't able to grieve for him, either. Husbands were either there, or they weren't; it was mostly a question of how many chops to buy for dinner. Their presence had no other significance; that was the message I brought with me from home.

So I'm totally unprepared for a person like Benny. There are days when I think he's invading my territory and forcing his way into my bedroom and lounge, days when I can't bear the sight of him. That never happened with Örjan; he was perfectly content to be somewhere on the sidelines, and I could put up with that.

And then there are the other days.

Desirée—I have trouble with that name. It sounds sharp, standoffish and hoity-toity, all those things I thought she was to begin with. I call her Shrimp. It fits her so well it's almost cruel. Pale, curled around her soft parts, with her shell on the outside. And long feelers.

There's so much about her I don't understand.

She spent a long time staring at a picture of my parents that I like a lot. They're lying sunbathing on a clifftop, seminaked, with their arms and legs all tangled together. They're lying cheek to cheek, eyes closed against the sun, smiling.

She found the picture distasteful, far too private.

"They are your parents, after all," she said. "Doesn't it ever strike you as a bit . . . well, too personal, a bit offensive?"

Offensive?

She's always freezing. I can never heat the place enough

for her, and while I'm feeling as if I'd like to tear my shirt off, she sits there in a sweater and thick socks. She loves me just sitting still, smoothing her hair with firm, regular strokes; then she curls up close beside me like a starving stray cat that's finally found a master.

But helpless and dependent are the last things she is! It's hard when I've counted on seeing her and she suddenly tells me she's changed her mind and is going to see a film with a good friend instead. Or when she knows I'm so busy and can't get away to see her in town, and she just says on the phone, "Okay then, might see you next week." Never, "Right, I'm coming over to your place!"

I want to reach her, and the truth of it is, I want to tie her down as well, but since she only seems to want me sometimes, I can't make any demands and that's so damn frustrating. And surely I could expect her to lend a hand in the house just occasionally! Or help me with the test milking or show a bit of interest in what I'm doing! I know I'm too used to women functioning as an extension of my own arm, and I wouldn't think of asking her to bake buns, but I still find it hard when she sits there with her nose in the newspaper while I'm running from job to job!

In fact, I wouldn't mind turning to bigamy—and getting together with Violet *and* Shrimp. Violet could be downstairs hemming curtains and curing salt beef, and in the bedroom I'd have Shrimp curling up against my chest and laughing her quiet, husky laugh. That laugh's become my reward and I'll do almost anything for it. It's like one of those "test your strength" machines they have at old fairgrounds. You have to hit a button with a heavy mallet, and then a marker runs up a scale. If you're really strong and hit the button hard enough, a bell rings.

Her laugh is that bell. And I don't often make it ring, but I've managed it a few times. And I can tell exactly whether I've got up to eighty on the scale, or missed the button entirely.

"You always like to be different, don't you, Benny?" Violet says in that disapproving tone. But she thinks I'm a real man, just like her Bengt-Göran, when I'm driving the big tractor with the tandem mounting or going out into the forest with my chainsaw in all my protective gear.

Shrimp's just the opposite. I can sense it's my "different" side that keeps her interested, and she just finds me tiresome when I put on my helmet and take a wad of chewing snuff.

How far has medical science advanced—could they transplant Shrimp's convoluted little beige soul into Violet's plump bosom and hardworking hands?

+✠+✠+✠+✠+✠+✠+✠+✠+✠+✠+✠+✠+✠+✠+✠+✠+✠+✠

Life, steaming and messy,
I've got the better of it,
I put labels on it, seal it in folders,
and file it in the archive

Something really upsetting happened today. Thinking about
it still makes me feel shaky.

Mrs. Lundmark didn't come to work today. That was
how it started.

It took a while for us to notice. She often gets here
before we do, hangs up her coat and her little fur hat in her
room, and creeps down into the store to—well, what does
she actually do when she isn't in the Children's section?
We all assume she's busy cataloguing, sorting, and clearing
things out, though nobody ever asks her, of course, and her
position in the library means none of us have any reason to
question her work. She spends more and more time in the
storeroom, just leaving a message for me or Britt-Mari to
look after Children's.

So we didn't notice until lunchtime. Mrs. Lundmark
always sits at the same table by the window and always eats

a bowl of soured milk with boring muesli while she reads one of the library service catalogues. If the whole room happens to go quiet, you can hear the wheezing of her airways, but apart from that you'd hardly notice her.

She sits there from 12:01 to 12:55. Then she gets to her feet, washes up her muesli bowl, and puts it on the draining rack. Then she goes to the toilet. We joke about it sometimes. Not many people have got a stomach you can set a clock by.

We're so used to it that she works a bit like a factory whistle now; we know it's lunchtime when she passes shelf X, the Sheet Music section outside the door of the staff room, and we start salivating like Pavlov's dogs. Sometimes it only takes the sound of her breathing to make us feel hungry. And when she gets up and goes over to the sink, having imbibed her soured milk in pointy little sips—she kisses it into her mouth from the tip of her spoon—we quickly bring our conversations to a close. We don't even need to look at our watches.

She didn't come to the staff room yesterday. She hadn't called in sick or booked a day's leave, either. We discussed the fact for maybe two minutes—and that was probably the most we've ever talked about her in all the time she's worked at this library. None of us has crossed her path, worked with her on any project, or had any kind of dispute with her. We haven't avoided her, either; we've chatted to her about the weather and our shift times every day—and for some reason she's always the one who organizes collections for colleagues who are leaving or having babies or celebrating special birthdays. Surprisingly, she has a knack for always choosing the ideal present—conventional, but exactly what the person wants. Well, for two minutes we wondered where she'd got to. Then we decided as usual that it was someone else's problem and plodded on with our own lives.

But she wasn't in the staff room today, either. So that made us talk about her for maybe three minutes. And then we did actually ask Olof if he knew anything about it. He didn't, and he said he didn't know anything about the way she organized her work, either. He'd once tried to discuss her duties with her, and she'd given him an explanation that took half an afternoon.

"Her cheeks went quite pink when I asked," Olof said, "and she ran off to fetch a ledger she kept, and then told me in great detail about a system she'd developed for when it was time to discard an item. In the end I had to say I'd got a dental appointment. I mean, how was I supposed to lead the conversation around from her ledger to Windows file handling?"

Mrs. Lundmark's absence didn't seem to have any impact at all on all the normal library routines. I often look after the Children's and Young People's section on my own these days, and I'm always grateful to her for giving me a free hand. No, that's far too nice a way of putting it: in actual fact, I thought I was more competent than she was, and it would have irritated me no end if she'd tried to interfere in how I was running things. So I suppose for me she's never been anything more than a not very functional piece of office furniture, one we could easily do without when we were next getting rid of things.

I rang her home number. An answering machine told me I was through to Inez Lundmark, who couldn't take my call just now. I cried, "Inez? Inez? It's me, Desirée!" several times in case she was there but hadn't bothered to pick up the phone, but I had no idea what sort of room my voice was echoing in, or even whether it was really okay to use her first name—I never had done before.

Now I'm no Good Samaritan. It would have been far more typical of us at work for Lilian to wring her hands and say "We must do something"—which all the rest of us would know meant us, not her. And Britt-Mari, with five children and less time than any of us, would have been the one to take action.

But it was that thing Olof said about claiming he had a dental appointment so he could get away from Mrs. Lundmark (Inez. Inez?) when she was explaining her system so eagerly. It gave me an ache somewhere in the region of my heart. Or rather, in the region of my gall bladder. A pressure, a vague sense of discomfort.

I asked Olof if I could take the time off to go around to where she lived. She hadn't phoned in sick, after all, and he didn't really know who to pass the problem on to, so he nodded, looking relieved. I went.

She lived in a big sooty block of flats with dark brickwork, which had seen better days. The stairwell was decorated with mock marble panels, and niches where statues had presumably once stood. Now, "Fuck your ass" was spray-painted inside them.

She opened her dark brown varnished front door at my first ring. She had a safety chain on the inside. She only hesitated a moment before unfastening it and letting me into her hall.

"Hello, Inez!" I said with a forced smile. "Are you all right? We were a bit worried at work."

She mumbled something and gestured limply toward the living room, and I followed her into a big bare room with filing cabinets along two of the walls. Filing cabinets?

"Do you live . . . on your own?" I asked. There was no easy way of saying, "And where do you keep Mr. Lundmark?"

"Back in the sixties they brought in the 'Mrs.' title for unmarried women, too," she said, jutting her chin forward. "I think it was the journalists who started it. Or maybe the health service, so unmarried mothers wouldn't feel any stigma."

What was I supposed to say? That none of us cared less whether she was Mrs. or Miss?

"I haven't been feeling quite right," she said after that. "Hope you'll excuse me. It'll soon pass, I expect."

Excuse her? What about reporting in sick, and the statutory waiting period before benefits payable, and doctors' certificates? She'd never been ill before, as far as I knew. Maybe she didn't even know there was more to it than just staying at home and saying sorry afterward. But then, I wasn't really there to represent authority.

She said no more.

"What have you got in your filing cabinets?" I asked, straight out.

She stared out of the window for a moment. It had fifties-style Venetian blinds, with plastic slats alternating in white and faded turquoise.

"You're a good girl," she said. "Much nicer than you think you are. So I can show you if you like."

And she did.

Two hours later, I stumbled down the worn and echoing stone steps from her apartment, choking back the tears. I had to talk to somebody, and for once Märta wasn't the obvious choice. She'd heard my descriptions of Mrs. Lundmark's ultraregular bowel movements all too often. I went to a telephone box and rang Benny.

No. 506 Amersfoort has hardly been able to put any weight on her left foreleg these last few weeks. Her hooves are as long as a cartoon cow's and I'm worried she might have hoof rot. It always makes me queasy just thinking about it, them standing there in the shit while the rot eats inward. Dad was always very careful about getting their hooves trimmed in good time, and when the hoofcare man came, I'd take over outside—but who the hell is there to take over from me?

Every day as I've battled to get the autumn plowing done, it's been in my mind to ring the farrier, but I've got to have the time to be his assistant, too. And one thing's for sure: going around dreaming about totally irrelevant stuff doesn't help one bit. Someone ought to tell her, Desirée, that her summer holiday smile almost made my best cow go lame.

I finally got hold of him; he came one afternoon and

we set to it. When we were indoors having a coffee, after several hours' work, Desirée rang. I closed the door to the kitchen and prepared myself to say a number of things not intended for the farrier's ears. But she hadn't rung for a chat. She was sobbing on the phone.

"I've got to come out and talk to you, right now," she said. "When does the next bus go?"

I felt a peculiar crawling sensation on my scalp. D-Day. She was about to tell me she'd had enough of me, more than enough, and then there'd be nothing left but 506 Amersfoort's hooves to occupy my time. Life would be sent back to Start, for me to play tedious new rounds forever and ever Amen.

I stood staring at myself in the hall mirror. A dirty old woolly hat, brown and orange. And under it, hair like handfuls of tow, a lot thinner than I remembered. Was this me? When had I last looked at myself in the mirror? Fancy her taking the trouble to come out on the bus to tell me in person! Great girl, that one.

Listlessly, I told her the bus times and dragged myself back out to the cowshed to finish the job. Then I did the milking, and just as I was putting out their silage, she came, with her toadstool hat pulled down over her ears and her hands thrust deep into her pockets. She climbed cautiously up onto the feeding platform and came trudging toward me, right up to me, jumping nervously aside whenever the cows tossed their heads. I put down the wheelbarrow and stood there, tense as a drawn bowstring.

She came up to me, put her arms around me, and rested her cheek against my filthy overalls.

"You're so normal," she said. "And you've got such a horrible old hat!"

She said it in the sort of tone she might've used for saying, "Listen darling, they're playing our song!"

I swear the cowshed instantaneously got lighter. It can do that sometimes, on late summer evenings when you turn off the hay drier and there's suddenly enough power for a few extra watts in the lights. It gets brighter, and you realize that yes, of course, this is how it should be!

She hadn't come to say she was through with me.

We went in and made some tea and had the rest of the cinnamon buns I'd bought for the farrier. Then she told me about her colleague at work going off the rails.

+X+X+X+X+X+X+X+X+X+X+X+X+X+X+X+X+X+X+X

I've grown out of my life
I need a new one
it doesn't matter if it's secondhand

Inez had bought her filing cabinets when the regiment was disbanded, sometime back in the seventies. She'd been stocking them with files for twenty years.

First, on the subject of her own family, unto the seventh generation. She got interested in genealogy. That was how it started, I later realized.

But why only collect information about people long since dead? She started putting together files on neighbors, colleagues, old classmates from school. She had no friends.

"I've never been interested in making any," she said matter-of-factly. "It only leads to all that tiresome give and take. You never have any freedom."

She had files on the checkout girl in the nearby Co-op, and on the landlord's agent, and the postman. They weren't very comprehensive.

"It's hard to find out things about them," she confided

apologetically. "Sometimes I make direct observations, and sometimes I get information from the births, marriages, and deaths columns in the paper. But I don't go to their homes."

"Direct observations?" I asked.

She gave a smile of satisfaction.

"You've never noticed, have you?" she said.

Noticed? Noticed what?

"I do a bit of spying," she said. "I'm not remotely interested in making any impact on people's lives; I don't want to harm anybody, or help anybody, either. And I've absolutely no intention of making any use of this information. The sort of material I collect is of no interest to most people, anyway. I've made an arrangement with a lawyer for all this to be shredded, unread, in the case of my death. But I'll let you see your own file."

She pulled out a green metal drawer marked "Colleagues" and extracted a hanging file. It was quite full.

"Sit!" she snapped, as if I were a particularly dozy dog. She put the file in front of me on the table.

There were black-and-white photos of me at the library, on a street in town, and on my balcony; the last of these seemed to be taken sideways from below, from the other side of the road. The photos from work were grainy, as if they'd been taken from a distance and enlarged.

"I've got developing equipment in the bathroom!" she said proudly.

There were lists of my work shifts, right up to today. There were circulars, minutes from union meetings, and memos I'd signed and sent around. There was a little notebook marked "Clothes" where she'd correctly recorded my favorite colors and fabrics, and made a few comments on things I'd worn: "Christmas party: red pleated skirt, long cardigan, blouse with a big collar." "May 15th: dark blue jacket, too big. Her late husband's?" There was a list of books I'd borrowed from the library and a couple of receipts from the supermarket where I shopped.

"They're your receipts!" she said. "Do you feel uncomfortable about me taking your picture without you knowing, and collecting up your receipts in the shop?"

I couldn't honestly say I did, especially not with her staring at me, head cocked to one side, as inscrutable as a house sparrow.

From the folder I took a large white handkerchief that smelled vaguely familiar. She blushed.

"Yes, it's yours!" she said. "I don't normally keep objects, but I wanted to preserve your perfume. It's Calvin Klein's Eternity, isn't it? That was what I decided, anyway, at the perfume counter in Domus."

"But you must do something with all this information you find out? Is it just because you like collecting and filing things? Or are you going to write a novel?" The idea suddenly came to me. I've read about writers who work like that.

"Not at all," she said irritably. "There are far too many novels already. But . . . well, sometimes . . . I try out your lives a bit, like you might try on clothes in a shop. Things you're not planning to buy at all, but you just fancy seeing yourself in something new! I might sit on the balcony and imagine I'm you, on your balcony, early one spring morning, in your old quilted jacket and your hat with the toadstools, eating some of those Finn Crisps you always buy. I shut my eyes and imagine my hair's straggly and white and I'm in my thirties. I mean, I would have made some preparations, bought the Finn Crisps, even been tempted to buy a bottle of Eternity! So I sit there and think about what I'm going to wear tomorrow; shall I choose my long green skirt or my sweater and jeans? Shall I go for lunch with my girl-friend or go to the cemetery? And then I think about my late husband; well, I often used to see him when he came to collect you! Not that I immerse myself in it or anything. I'm not all that interested in your actual feelings."

"My file's bulging," I mumbled. "I can see you haven't got anything like as much on Lilian."

"Her life doesn't interest me as much. I've just got a few external observations, because I might happen to catch sight of her when I'm being someone else. And she has to have birthday presents, too, of course!"

Birthday presents! No wonder she was so good at choosing just the right present!

"I'm quite interested in you, on the other hand," said Inez. "You seem to be someone else who observes, more than you take part. But I think you're too impatient to file away what you see. Maybe, if you give it time."

She sounded like a patient primary school teacher. Given time, you could be stark raving mad, too, dear! But was she?

"Can you tell me anything about my life that I don't know?" I asked, all of a sudden.

"Yes," she replied. "But I'm certainly not going to. That would be cheating. And it could be dangerous. It would feel like one of those science fiction stories, you know, where somebody accidentally alters some little detail in the past and completely changes the present. Well, I don't know. But I do know I'm really just trying out your life for brief spells, now and then. Just borrowing it. I don't wear it out!"

I once heard a Finnish scientist say that normal just means someone who hasn't yet been studied in sufficient detail. Why was it any crazier to map out people's lives than to go birdwatching? No, she was no more mad than I was, and neither bitter nor sentimental. Just practical and efficient and very poetic.

"That new man," she said. "He puzzles me. He's either completely wrong for you, or the only conceivable one."

"Benny? Oh, Inez, what shall I do about Benny?"

"I most certainly do not hand out advice!" said Inez.

Something happened, around about the time she came out and told me about that colleague of hers. It was as if after that she started opening her eyes more often than her mouth. It's hard to describe.

Of course, she tended to talk a lot. And I wasn't one to object—considering the silence I'd been living in. I found most of what she said interesting, or fun, or sweet, or something. But I did sometimes wonder if it was possible for her to experience anything without talking about it simultaneously. It seemed to be her way of absorbing what she saw, as if she had to grind it up small to be able to swallow it, like pensioners with bad teeth.

There are people who use cameras like that, you know. Once when I was little, we went on vacation to Gothenburg for three days, with Mum's cousin Birgitta. And Birgitta spent all her time taking pictures: the botanical gardens, the harbor, the funfair at Liseberg, the tour boats, and the trams. Somehow she didn't enjoy anything unless she could take a picture of it. And then that winter, when she'd come to visit and we all sat talking about the trip and looking at her album, she turned out not to remember a single thing she hadn't got a shot of, not even that daft waiter in the hotel restaurant who could waggle his ears. It must be hell for Birgitta if one of her films doesn't come out—like losing a few months of her life. She didn't even take particularly good pictures.

Shrimp was a little bit like that. She had to talk about everything. And there was really only one place where it bothered me: in bed. Because even as she was fondling me to the point where I felt quite giddy, she'd be talking, sometimes about what we were doing, and that made me feel a bit embarrassed: "Mm, wonder if the elbow's an acknowledged erogenous zone, or if it's you making it into one? . . . Did you know the Duchess of Nivers drew a map of her private parts and painted it in watercolors, so her lovers would find it easier to satisfy her?"

She'd go on like that. And I could never find anything to say.

Until that evening when she'd been with the old lady and her filing cabinets. At first she didn't seem very interested in doing anything at all, even though she said she wanted to stay the night. She got undressed and lay down on my bed, flat on her back, and stared silently at the ceiling. But since it always still feels like Christmas for me just having her here, I couldn't keep my hands off her.

Sometimes I think I'm trying to learn her body by heart, as if it was going to disappear. I know the hollows behind her collarbone, her straight little toes, the birthmark under her left breast, and the white fuzz on her forearms. If we'd been playing blind man's bluff, I'd never have mistaken her for anyone else, at least not if she was naked. I think, in fact, I could recognize her just from the way her nose turns up. The funny thing about her is, she thinks she's completely uninteresting. I've no idea if she's ugly or beautiful; it's kind of irrelevant. As long as she's her.

That evening she didn't say a word. I didn't know if I could start making love to her or not; she usually gives me a clear signal when she thinks it's time. But then she gave a big sigh and pushed me down onto my back, took my hands and crossed them on my chest. And then she started playing blind man's bluff with me, still in complete silence.

They say lonely people go to the hairdresser's and the dentist's and the chiropractor's when they don't need to, just to feel someone's touch. She'd never touched me like that before—and it was nothing to do with erogenous zones. Not for a while, at any rate. I think I was on the verge of tears. And I know she was crying. Her tears were falling onto my hand, but when I tried to say something, she put her finger over my mouth.

"Shhh, I'm trying out my life!" she said. I don't know what she meant, but just then it seemed so obvious, like it does in a dream.

❉✠❉✠❉✠❉✠❉✠❉✠❉✠❉✠❉✠❉✠❉✠❉✠❉✠❉✠❉

> *Your caressing hands*
> *give me shoulders and breasts.*
> *You give me foot arches, earlobes,*
> *and a little squirrel between my thighs.*

He's got a couple of little chicken-pox scars on his face, one on his temple and one at the corner of his mouth. Right in the middle of a complicated computer search for reference material at work this morning, I found myself stroking the keyboard with my index finger as if it were his face and his scars. I closed my eyes and traced them across from *P* to *D*, caressed the slightly concave keys with my fingertip, then opened my eyes and looked at my hands as if I'd never seen them before. Those bony white fingers know the down on his neck bones, the hollows at his collarbone, and the twisting veins on his forearms, and they've followed the line of hair from his navel and down. . . .

Existence has become so physical I feel I'm losing my grip on it. People have told me that when they stopped smoking, they could suddenly appreciate how fragrant tea was, how cream tasted, how springtime was a whole composition of scents. My tactile corpuscles seem to have taken that leap; I can feel a chair soft and well sprung beneath my thigh; the roughness of linen to the touch, a precise little sensation if you run a feather across your lips. If it goes on like this, people will start tapping their heads knowingly and rolling their eyes to heaven whenever I start fingering the things around me.

I had to ring Märta. When I told her I'd been stroking my computer keyboard, she made such a strange sound, a sort of low, warm, protective cooing, seeming to express how pleased she was for me. But all she said was that I should watch out I didn't get myself arrested for sexual harassment of office equipment.

I've never been a particularly sensual person; life with Örjan taught me that. I took it with equanimity, in fact, I may even have been proud of it, as if it made me a rational being, above more carnal behavior. The tabloids' Sunday sex supplements made me snort in irritation: apply pressure here and rotate your tongue there, sometimes concluding with an "and that's the way to keep him loving you . . ."; it all seemed so clinically efficient, like a course in retiling your bathroom using the best possible technique for getting the edges flush. I mean, there's nothing wrong with courses in efficiency and effectiveness, but don't try telling me they've got anything to do with Love. I refused to embark on a career as a member of the harem; I got quite enough of being efficient at work.

And Örjan understood, and was more than happy to take the role of Husband who always wants a Bit More than his wife; I made him seem more potent by being less than hot myself. What would he have done if I, wild with hunger, had put out a foot and felled him on the hall rug? I think

111

he'd have wilted instantly. Looking back, I'm not convinced he was so very sensual himself.

Because he'd never have shown such childish impatience as Benny sometimes does, when we haven't seen each other for a while. As if he'd been standing for ages with his nose pressed to the sweet shop window, longing himself almost to death with his pocket money in his hand. He's really gone over me comprehensively, every square centimeter, with all five senses and sometimes even the sixth, or that's the way it feels. He can find birthmarks I never knew existed, nose into the back of my knee or lie looking at a nipple as if he's never seen one before. He gets a bit uncomfortable when I laugh at him, and tells me it's a professional thing: he's so used to assessing udders . . . but there's no mistaking his eagerness and pleasure, or his wish for me to share them with him.

When he first started his voyages of discovery, I was really rather embarrassed, and asked him if he was giving me my annual physical. But in fact, that was mainly because I felt so stupidly, unexpectedly shy. I don't know when I embarked on my own investigations of him, but from that moment, of course, we found twice as much, and my hands started feeling empty when I hadn't got him to occupy them.

Sometimes when I look at his lips and think about where they've been, my face still flushes well and truly red. Me! Who prescribed myself regular doses of lovers as vitamin pills to keep my system in shape.

We're usually at my place, because its trickier for me to get away, but now and then we spend an evening at her apartment. I don't like it there at all. The walls are white, the carpets are white, the few items of furniture she's got are all tubular metal ones. It feels like being in a bloody hospital ward. She stands there in the kitchen cooking some vegetable concoction that gives me wind. Before I know it, somebody'll stick their head around the door and say, "Do come in. The doctor will see you now!"

In the corner she's got some potted plants as tall as young birches. For all I know, they could be plastic; the whole apartment seems to have been sanitized of anything that could give you allergies. The only thing that brightens it up is that poster I bought her. It's pretty silly, so it's nice of her to have kept it.

Maybe I should give her some of Mum's cross-stitch pictures? God knows, I've got more than enough. I think

Mum must have produced one a week for fifty years; most of them she found a use for as birthday presents for friends and neighbors. I can go anywhere in the village and find her nimble handiwork staring me in the face from some corner or other. And yet there are still enough left at home for me to wallpaper the whole house; there's a trunkful in the attic.

She hasn't got a television. No VCR, either, of course. So I avoid going over if there's a big match—but naturally I don't tell her that. Those evenings it's "absolutely vital to get some paperwork done." Once she came to my place instead, and then, of course, I had to miss the match and wrestle with Dad's bureau and all its overflowing piles of paper. And it was a bloody good job I did. I found Overdraft here and Threat of Debt Collection there, Final Deadline for Payment, and Despite Repeated Reminders. I sat up half the night sweating over it, and did actually get through most of the backlog. Perhaps she's a kind of guardian angel, without knowing it.

And it was amazing sitting there frowning over my current account balance while she was slinking onto my lap and exploiting me shamelessly. With those sort of professional perks, I could well imagine myself becoming a very hardworking and conscientious accountant . . . well, all right, we don't always manage to save ourselves for our late-night sessions of blindman's bluff. I mean to say, I've got a cowshed to drag myself to at dawn each day.

I asked her why she hasn't got a television. When she's at my place, she has no inhibitions about goggling at everything, especially the advertisements. Her favorites are those pudgy babies lisping about their snug-fitting diapers. She watches everything wide-eyed, from chat shows with studio audiences of happy pensioners who collect garden gnomes, to late-night thrillers that always end with somebody driving off a high cliff. I've made love to her on the deep-pile rug in front of the TV set without her even dragging her eyes away from *Friends*.

"You see!" she said. "It would be hopeless for a person like me to have a television!"

The only thing she can't stand is sports. As soon as she hears the theme tune of a sports program, she groans with irritation and digs out some flipping poetry book from her flowery fabric bag. She never goes anywhere without it, and she's always got a couple of books in there.

Or she does whatever she can to distract me. I've been straddled by her on the deep-pile rug without taking my eyes off the Björklöven-Modo match.

A couple of times we rented a movie. Or rather, we've never rented just one, because we can never agree. We rent two. Then she gets out her flowery bag while my movie's on, and I fall asleep during hers.

We're like chalk and cheese, as Mum and Dad used to say. And I don't want it ever to end. I'll just have to take it one day at a time.

✦✖✦✖✦✖✦✖ ✦✖✦✖✦✖✦✖✦✖✦✖✦✖✦ ✦✖✦✖✦✖✦✖■

Okay then
You're the one with the bucket and spade
but I've got all the nice baking tins

Occasionally I ask him if he wants me to borrow anything from the library for him, since he hasn't time to go in person. "If you've read one book, you've read them all, and I read one last year!" he says, with a silly, cross-eyed look.

Sometimes I manage to talk him into going to a film, and just as he's plodding determinedly into *Police Academy 14*, I divert him into *The Piano*. He watches the film morosely for a bit. During the love scenes in the swamp, he lets his fingers creep down between my thighs until I'm squirming like a maggot on a hook. "I'm missing the sports news right this minute!" he hisses in my ear.

On our way out, he makes such a fuss that people start turning around: "People in the old days weren't such clumsy idiots! They'd have had the sense to dig a proper landing place, not just hurled the piano around the beach any old how!"

Once, and only once, I drag him along to the theater

116

with me. It's a noirish, avant-garde play with lots of short scenes meant to illustrate the emptiness of modern city life; he whinnies audibly in the deathly quiet of the auditorium. "Haven't enjoyed myself this much since I saw *101 Dalmatians*," he announces loudly in the foyer, and gives me a defiant stare.

"You only do it to provoke me!" I roar at him in the hamburger bar afterward. "No one could call you deranged or mentally deficient. So why is it you can't bear me having an existence of my own, or admit there's something of value in it? I don't come along and make stupid comments about your disc harrow!"

"But then I've never expected you to sit and stare at it for two hours," he says indignantly. Silence descends.

To get me back, he drags me along to something called Tractor Pulling the Sunday after. Gigantic tractors are competing to pull heavy weights and spewing out dirty blue diesel fumes into the clear autumn air. The noise is appalling. It would have made Örjan burst into a series of angry articles. I feel ill, and ill at ease, in every possible way. Benny pulls his forest owner's cap farther down his nose and totally ignores me while he talks carburetors with other blokes in caps.

Then we go home and make mad, passionate love.

"Is that all it's about?" I whine to Märta.

"Whaddya mean, 'all'?" she says.

The very best times are when we lie there all tangled together afterward, calm and relaxed. We often invent little tests to find out more about each other.

"What would you do if you were standing eyeball to eyeball with a bull on the loose?" he asks.

"I'd make a fantastic five-meter leap to reach a fence, then pass out just before I managed to climb over it, and be gored to a pulp," I say.

"Oh no, you wouldn't. You'd go up to the bull and tell him sternly he wasn't to molest women in public, and the bull would pass out!" he says.

"What do you do if you suddenly discover you've been going around at a posh party with your fly undone and selected bits hanging out?" I ask.

"I'd get out the whole lot and say I've been sent by the National Flashers' Association and ask people if they'd like to support our work with a small financial contribution," he answers straightaway. "No, in real life I'd try to pull up the zip without anyone noticing, but get the tablecloth caught in it and pull all the plates onto the floor. Then I'd back toward the door with the cloth hanging from my fly, grinning from ear to ear, trip over the cloth as I edged out, fall downstairs, and break both legs! What would you do if you'd gone and bought a book, then went in another bookshop where the assistant suspected you of shoplifting it?"

"I'd pay for it all over again with a hysterical laugh, and what's more, I'd buy three more copies of the same book and go wittering on about it being so good I wanted to give it to all my friends. And then leave the shop with bright red ears, accidentally leaving all four copies behind on the counter!"

We agree that if he's the Prize Loser of all Sweden, I could be the Prize Loser, and end up sharing the same glass case at the folk museum, stuffed just like him.

In the winter months it's not quite so hectic on the farm. I should really have been doing some forestry work, of course, but a lot of loose, wet snow fell in November and it was hard to get about. Or so I convinced myself. It was raw, icy cold and windy, too—the sort of weather no amount of wrapping up can keep out.

I felt a real urge to do something to the old house. I don't mean fancy carved woodwork on the front porch, mind you; that's way down on my to-do list. But . . .

I saw a program the other day about some fifties' gas stations that are listed historic buildings. And suddenly it hit me that they could just as well have listed my living room. The kitchen, too. Mum was never really interested in home decorating. She kept the place clean, all right, but otherwise she was happy to leave most things the way they were in her parents' time, and she could never bear to get rid of anything she and Dad had bought together. And me?

The only room in the house I've ever felt any urge to

decorate is my own. There was this time when I was about seventeen, just before I had to take over the farm: I went at Grandma's drab old brown wallpaper and painted it black all over! I put a tigerskin rug on the bed and posters on the walls, of hard rock stars with big hair, plus one of a naked girl with jointing instructions, her body divided up by blue pencil lines. It seemed incredibly daring, back then. God, I was cool! And Carina thought I was cool, too. One midsummer's eve, when my parents were away and I was going to do the morning milking, I smuggled her up to my room and tried to draw the same diagram on her. In marker pen. We were both quite drunk, on something that could well have made us go blind. And by the time we'd had a good roll around on the tigerskin rug, it looked pretty disgusting; Mum threw it out without asking any questions. She was like that.

Later on, I took down the rock stars and put up pictures of monster tractors. But I never got around to redecorating the room. Desirée said once it made her feel as if she were lying in a crypt whenever she looked at the black walls. And that was when I got to thinking I ought to change a few things in the house. I suppose I started feeling some kind of nesting instinct when she came into my life. I should have known better. The whole subject turned out to be a minefield.

First, I rewallpapered my room in a very nice flowery pattern. Then I sent off for some ready-made curtains from the Halén's catalogue, white with lots of frills, and shiny ribbons to bunch them up at the side of the window. I finished it off with a couple of Mum's cross-stitch pictures of flowers, in place of the tractors.

I did it when I knew there was a whole week before her next visit. And when she did come, I took her up to the bedroom, flung open the door, and tried to sound like a trumpet fanfare.

She stared. "Oh . . . very nice!" was all she said.

I just stood there, crestfallen. And then I tried to prod her into saying more, to tell me how clever I'd been, to . . .

To say she knew she was going to be really happy in this bedroom.

But all I could get her to say was that it was much lighter now, and seemed bigger.

"But don't you think it looks nice?" I prompted.

I shouldn't have asked. Desirée isn't much of a one for lies, even the white kind. She just said that it was quite right for me to decorate the room according to my own taste, not hers.

"Do you mean you wanted to be there to help choose the wallpaper?" I said, before I could stop myself.

So that really brought the whole thing to a head, though I didn't realize it at the time. A question that had come far too early. Because all she said was, "No, why would I?," then went down to switch on the television because she didn't want to miss the news.

Then there was an atmosphere all evening. We started arguing about the news. She's sort of left-wing: not exactly a champagne socialist, more an herbal tea lefty; and I defend the employers because I see myself as a small businessman. She wastes no time trapping me in a position where I find myself defending international big business, and since she's so much more used to arguing than I am, she gets me to say things I don't even agree with. And then I lose my temper and out it all comes: I defend industrial-scale tree felling and pour scorn on naive field biologists; she holds forth passionately on the destruction of the environment and exploitation of the earth's resources, and I practically accuse her of being an animal rights activist who sets fire to meat trucks.

And all the while, I can sense that this argument's really about bedroom wallpaper. She wants to pick a quarrel because she doesn't want to confront the question of whether what happens in this house is anything to do with her.

For the first time, we go to sleep without making love first.

But we hold hands.

I love select simplicity,
clean lines, muted colors . . .
A summer meadow in flower
is actually a bit much

I had to fight back a violent urge to giggle when I first saw
the curtains, which looked like a ball gown from *Gone with
the Wind*, and realized the cross-stitch pictures had invaded
the last sanctuary in the house, his own, dear old crypt. But
he was standing there bursting with pride; I felt my spirits
sink and was lost for words. I had absolutely no intention
of expressing any opinion on his decorating tastes—
because it would have implied I thought I should have a say
in the matter. And that was an issue I didn't want to touch
with a barge pole. Not yet.

And then all that silly bickering in front of the television! At the time I was quite elated as I lured him into one
trap after another, but later I was on the verge of tears. The
last thing I wanted was for him to blurt out all those reactionary clichés so I'd lose all respect for him. Especially
since I know he's neither stupid nor reactionary. And he's

knowledgeable in areas where I've never even set foot. But if you're on different stars there's nothing to be done.

There've been other times when it's taken a more good-humored form.

Another area where we disapproved of each other, for example, was our clothes.

One day he turned up at my place with a shopping bag from Diana's Modes, a place where fifty-something female executives buy tailored three-piece skirt suits, navy blue with chic little scarves. And draped party numbers for special occasions, with sequined embroidery spreading like eczema across their chests. Märta and I often take a look in their window for a laugh.

"They had a sale!" he said proudly. "Go on, open it!"

Not a skirt suit, not a party number. But a horrendous, flared, "girly" skirt with gigantic mauve roses and fluorescent green leaves. I could conceivably have hung it on the wall at home and called it an installation. But be seen wearing it in public? Not on your life!

"But . . . it's not me!" I ventured, trying not to hurt his feelings.

Wasted effort. He understands things instantly. So then I elaborated, not wanting him to think I was being hypocritical. "It's . . . well, dreadful, actually."

He'd definitely have preferred me to be hypocritical.

"Why do you always have to dress so you look like a drowned corpse that's just been washed up?" he snarled, stuffing the skirt back into the shopping bag. "Take the bloody thing, anyway. You can always tear it into rags and use it to clean the windows!"

"Drowned corpse!" I was speechless. "Take it yourself. Just in case you ever get around to cleaning any windows!

Or wear it in the cowshed; the smell couldn't make it any worse than it already is!"

We glared at each other.

Then he sat down heavily on his hands, beside me on the sofa.

"I don't hit people smaller than me!" he said through gritted teeth. "I don't, I don't!"

"I do shove them, though," he added, pushing me so I fell over on the sofa. He pulled off my T-shirt, made of unbleached, organically grown cotton. "Come to think of it, you always look best without clothes. Or without your own clothes, at any rate. I've never seen anything worse than your hairy wool hat with toadstools!"

I'd had time to spot that he'd paid quite a lot of money for the skirt, and I knew he didn't have money to burn. So I decided we'd go out to the shops, where I'd buy him some item of clothing that cost the same, as a gesture of reconciliation. The choice would be mine, and if he didn't like it, he'd have the pleasure of telling me so, to my face. Then we'd be even.

We wandered around department stores for several hours, until he had to dash off back to the cowshed as usual. I fingered soft Mulberry flannel shirts: small checks in eggshell shades or tobacco brown. Perfect casual wear for the country squire! "I buy those from the catalogue in bargain three-packs, to wear in the cowshed!" he grumbled. A delicious French shirt designed to be worn open almost to the waist made him laugh uproariously. "I'd be sure to get lots of offers in that one!" he said. "From other guys!"

Like a hunting dog on a leash, he kept tugging me toward racks of garishly patterned shirts with matching ties, and jackets in weird styles that might have been all the rage in Hollywood ten years ago. When it came to "smart" clothes for town, he favored the pimp look. As for work clothes, it wasn't done to buy them in shops at all; you got them from a mail-order catalogue and charged them to the farm account.

In the end I had to settle for a T-shirt like the one I was wearing, which he blithely promised to wear next time he had to clean the manure spreader.

"Do you mind if I snoop in your cupboards and drawers?" she said.

I thought I probably hadn't got much to hide, apart from the odd porn magazine, which I'd be prepared to justify if it came to it.

But she found something much worse.

She found my final report and exam marks from upper secondary school.

She looked through all my good grades with her mouth dropping wide open, almost down to her little plums of breasts. She got excited and started stuttering that if I didn't mind her saying so, it was shameful my parents hadn't let me carry on with my studies. With results like that! She started driveling on about adult education and grants and courses for mature students.

That was the first time I was really, blazingly angry

with her. I felt like punching her right in the middle of her pale eggshell face until her nose bled. But in our family we simply don't hit women. Nothing to do with chivalry, though; it's more that we don't want to damage a valuable part of the labor force.

But I did want to hit her, and you could hardly call her part of the labor force.

Instead, I pulled on my jacket and ran out without a word, right in the middle of her ranting. I went to the cowshed to check on a cow with postpartum paralysis who had just started trying to get up from the pallet in her stall. I was so agitated that my hands were shaking as I stroked the sweaty ridge of hair along her head, while she struggled up. At last she managed to get all four legs straight and stood munching her extra scoops of concentrated feed. I rested my forehead against her side. "Don't give up!" I whispered. "Don't give up! Don't give up!"

Then I went back in.

Miss Desirée, the Much Desired, gave an irritable snort.

"Can't you leave your cowshed clothes in the cellar?" she said. "Anyway, those residential courses for mature students . . ."

I clenched my fists and pressed them to my ears.

"D'you realize what you're saying? You're telling me to sell the farm!" I shouted. "Because I don't suppose you were thinking of running the place while I live the high life on my mature student's grant? Or were you maybe thinking I'd take the cows along with me and keep them in the student accommodation?"

She turned paler still, more white than beige.

"I don't know what you're getting so worked up about," she muttered. "There must be some way you could study, if you felt like it. I just meant you seem to have the brains for it. But maybe you don't want to. Forget I mentioned it!"

"Want!" I roared. "Oh yeah, I might want! And what then? When I've spent five or six years studying and building up an extra half million kronor in student loan repayments to add to the debts I've already got? Become a librarian maybe, and mince around the shelves thinking about my posh qualifications? And what the hell do you know about what my parents 'let' me do!"

She sat in complete silence, her eyes fixed on my school report. I snatched it away from her, tore it into tiny pieces and let them shower down over her head. I totally lost it.

"You couldn't care less what I 'want'!" I bellowed. "You do all the wanting yourself. Wanting somebody to talk Lackong with, so you needn't feel ashamed in front of your library friends. And you don't understand a pissing thing about what having a farm means. What I want is somebody to help me make sure the cows who've just calved get their Paragel in time, so they don't lie down and give up!"

I was shouting, louder and louder.

She stood up.

"Who exactly are you trying to shout down?" was all she said as she slipped out of the room. I heard the car start in the yard, then there was a deafening silence. And the question hung in the air.

I leave no impression in the water;
in the class photo I'm what-was-she-called
and my gold earrings will be inherited by the state

I've never felt so bad in all my life.

And I was so pleased to start with. His final report card, which I found at the back of a drawer, sandwiched between a swimming certificate and a cutaway diagram of a moped motor, confirmed what I'd been suspecting all along. Top grades in almost everything—Swedish, Math, English. He'd only dropped a grade in two subjects—Religious Education and Handicraft. There was a good head on those shoulders. He'd never had time to be any kind of scholar; I knew he'd had to start helping on the farm almost as soon as he could walk. That was probably what made him do his uneducated peasant act every time I tried to force any highbrow culture down his throat. It was a provocation to him. He knew he'd be capable of getting something out of it, and if he ever let it near him, he'd be forced to admit he'd missed something. Made the "wrong" choice.

I was totally unprepared for his furious outburst. There seemed nothing I could say. I'd only been trying to get to know him better, and I'd imagined we might find a few stars to build that bridge with. Gold stars.

I had tears of self-pity in my eyes as I put my foot down and zoomed off. Oh, how misunderstood I was.

Of course I wasn't anything of the kind! It was me who'd got entirely the wrong end of the stick, as I realized by about six that evening after fourteen cups of tea. The girl who'd always got gold stars in her own little book. And praise from Mummy. Clever Desirée who was going to shine the light of Education and Culture into his rural darkness. It was quite true: I didn't know a pissing thing about what his parents had asked of him. All I knew was that they were dead and he'd set up a whole garden center on their grave.

Suddenly I was longing desperately for my own mother, so much so that I even longed for Daddy a little bit, too. For the big oak table, an heirloom, where I used to sit and read aloud to Mummy from my English book, with wildly exaggerated pronunciation. She didn't speak English, but she made sure I went to England on a language course every summer. She cried the first time I faltered my way through a Mozart sonatina on the piano. She couldn't decide if she wanted me to be a concert pianist or just a Nobel prizewinner in whatever field I chose.

A librarian was what I became, with a very modest salary and several hundred thousand owing on my student loan. But so well read. No longer played the piano but could now perform "Jingle Bells" on the mouth organ. I was the obvious choice to preach to Big Benny of Rowan Farm.

I didn't dare answer the phone the next day. I was afraid

it might be Benny. And I was even more afraid it might not be Benny. So I took three days' leave and told Daddy I'd be coming home.

Some people say they can tell you the precise moment when they grew up. Märta says it was when she found her mum in bed with the red-haired man next door. Märta's the only redhead in her family.

For me it was during that visit home.

Not that I uncovered any family secrets. If there were any, they're long buried under the inland ice sheet. And nothing particularly unexpected happened, really. Daddy had reluctantly foregone a Rotary meeting and told me peevish tales about the uselessness of the sluts they sent him as care workers. In between, he said nothing. He didn't ask a single question about how things were going in my life, and all he said about Mummy was, "She'll just have to put up with the way things are. I haven't the energy to be running around there all the time, and she certainly can't count on you!"

Oh yes, she can, I thought, while I'm here she can count on me. I shall go there and see if her hands still feel the way I remember them.

I went to visit her on all three days. Once she smiled at me and said, "Oh, have you got a free period, dear?" Apart from that, I didn't understand very much of what she said, though she said quite a lot. Her head was like a malfunctioning telephone exchange; she kept answering the wrong calls.

On the train home, it occurred to me that if I had to fill in a form and give my next of kin, I might as well leave the space blank. And if I got up in the night to go to the toilet on the train, opened the wrong door and fell out into the darkness, it would make very little difference to the world.

I worked like mad for several days, so I wouldn't be in if the phone rang. I even went out and cleared a new area of trees, though I generally try not to work alone in the forest; I know of too many people who've ended up trapped under trees that fell the wrong way, or crawling through the woods with their leg half-sawn through. And then I thought: if that happened to me, who'd put the death announcement in the paper? I imagined the world's longest death announcement, signed by twenty-four cows with their names and numbers.

But I'm not a babe in the wood, lost and all alone; I know that. It would soon be Christmas, and at least ten lots of people had asked me to come over and spend it with them. My relations, of course, but they don't live that locally, and they know I can't really bring the cows along with me. And then various families in the village. An old couple who were Mum's closest friends and have no children of their own—they'd flutter around me like delighted sparrows if I turned up there on Christmas Eve. And Bengt-Göran and Violet, no doubt; they took it for granted I'd be with them, and I supposed I would. Violet's Christmas buffet took some beating!

I tried to avoid the thought of me and Shrimp twinkling together in front of a Christmas tree. And eating brawn—from a shop, not the traditional homemade—straight out of the plastic wrapper. Or some flipping lentil soup!

Mum and I used to invite the family over. Even last year we did; she was allowed home from the hospital for a couple of days, and Auntie Ingrid and my cousin Anita turned up with their car trunks full of food. There were eleven of us. We all knew it was Mum's last Christmas, but we had a really good time, strange though it may sound. Anita's a nurse at the county hospital, and before that she worked in Switzerland for quite a few years. She told us stories about her time there, and then the air was thick with tall tales, childhood memories, and worn-out family jokes. We even laughed when Uncle Greger did his same old imitation of Evert Taube singing. And as the night wore on, Mum said craftily: "Well, maybe we should leave the youngsters on their own for a while!" She meant me and Anita. And we sat there obediently, drinking brandy mixed with Christmas root beer until half past four on Christmas morning, and Anita told me how she'd got pregnant by a married Swiss doctor and had an abortion.

I didn't bother putting up any Christmas decorations in the house this year. I sat morosely at the kitchen table, staring around the kitchen.

Mum would have despaired. I was letting the place go;

it already had the air of an abandoned farmhouse or a hostel for old bachelors. I'd repainted the veranda railing and replaced the guttering—but I didn't know where to start when it came to fancy touches indoors. I did the basic cleaning up, but I couldn't go starching little cloths or putting friezes of Santa's elves along the kitchen shelves like Mum used to at Christmas.

The old couple gave me a plastic basket with two spindly pink hyacinths and a big box of Aladdin chocolate assortments as a thank-you for cutting the grass in their fallow pasture for them. And I'd bought a box of red candles on special offer. Once I put a few of those in the candleholders and lit them, at least I didn't have to see the rest of the kitchen. The television went on as soon as I got in, and droned away festively to itself in a corner. I'd brought it into the kitchen.

Two days before Christmas Eve, at ten in the evening, Shrimp rang.

"It's me. Can I spend Christmas with you?" she said.

"Of course you can spend Christmas with me!" I said.

And the next day I drove in to fetch her.

We're like two shaggy bears you and I, my friend,
as we crawl into our lair and dream of summer without end.
Forget people's din, their gloomy buildings encroaching
to dream of silent forests and the midnight sun approaching

Piercing icy winds and darkness deepening day by day—
come and lie close and warm yourself here by me!
Far off a wolf howls, the waiting hunter defies the storm.
Let me hide my muzzle in your fur so rough and warm!

Märta and her Passion had invited me around for Christmas
Eve. As I mentioned, the Passion's name is Robert—Märta
calls him Robertino, Bobby, or Bloody Bob, depending on
how she's feeling about him at that particular moment
and whether he's done anything to humiliate her lately.
Robert's forty-five and he's got dark hair combed across
a bald patch and could charm the panties off a shop-
window dummy—I mean that sincerely. And he's always
ready to exercise his charm on me, too.

Several of my library colleagues who live alone or are
single parents had decided to get together for Christmas

Eve at a place you could rent outside town, and all bring something for the buffet. I'd been one of the keenest promoters of the idea. Robertino with a few glasses of mulled wine inside him was more than I could cope with.

I went out shopping to get some little Christmas gifts for them and their children.

But I came home with a bagload of presents for Benny. It took me until that evening to realize every single thing I'd bought was for him. I tried to convince myself I'd bought them for the children, or a Merry Band of Partygoers, but all I had in my head was what Benny would think of them. At that point, I gave in and rang to ask if I could spend Christmas with him. He said yes straightaway; I think we were both pretty surprised. I rang off and then I had a little cry, as I saw in my mind's eye a train door gaping wide in the darkness.

The next day he came to fetch me and we did the rounds of the crowded Domus store. Märta had lent me an old, grease-stained copy of the *Swedish Princesses' Cookbook* from the thirties, and I bought the ingredients for Superior Toffee 1, Crisp Doughnut Twists, Stuffed Pork Ribs (Mock Goose), and Herring à la Russe. I had a couple of other schemes, but had to abandon them when I couldn't find potash, brewer's wort, or full-cream milk in the supermarket section. Benny was all for Pork Brawn, but the recipe called for a pig's head, so he transferred his enthusiasm to Lung Hash. He claimed he could provide the calf's pluck. While I was hunting for potash among all the exotic chutney mixes in the spice display, Benny sneaked off and came back with a bag he wouldn't let me open. Then we drove back to Rowan Farm.

We turned on the fluorescent light in the kitchen, tied

tea towels around our heads and waists, propped the *Swedish Princesses' Cookbook* against the television, and set to work.

Superior Toffee 1 went well. We'd forgotten to buy sweet cases, of course, but Benny reckoned he could easily make his own from greaseproof paper, the way it showed you in the book. We poured the delicious-smelling mixture into his crumpled little creations and felt very pleased with ourselves. Crisp Doughnut Twists proved more of a challenge. "If the dough is worked for too long, air bubbles will form!" Benny quoted sternly, setting an egg timer for two minutes.

So far so good, but when we came to the part where you were supposed to pass one end through a lengthways slit before pulling it into a knot, we came totally unstuck.

"Just give me a princess and we'll see how she likes having one end passed through a lengthways slit before being pulled into a knot!" Benny roared.

I, meanwhile, was battling with Stuffed Pork Ribs (Mock Goose) and whining on about Preshrunk Twine and Larding Needles. If the truth be told, we were both getting pretty talkative and inclined to take shortcuts with the cooking, because we were knocking back the mulled wine more or less continuously. We also had a very lively discussion about who was actually mock, the poor pork ribs trying to look like goose, or the poor goose who'd never asked for its name to be used. I took the ribs' side, Benny, the goose's.

The Herring à la Russe looked very attractive, a bit like an early Niki de Saint Phalle, one of those where she baked colored paint into plaster and used a shotgun to spray out a work of art.

By half past eleven that evening, the kitchen pretty

much resembled the cowshed—though it smelled better, Benny said, and promptly fell asleep on the kitchen banquette. I cleared up as best I could, and had the satisfaction of feeling generations of exhausted housewives lining up behind me.

Then I dragged him up to bed. And he was drunk! I was, too, of course, which slightly spoiled my exhausted housewife image. He woke up and grumbled when I dropped him on the stairs, but then went peacefully back to sleep. I collapsed headlong beside him and stared with inebriated concentration at his floral wallpaper; I even felt a sentimental tenderness for those ball gown curtains.

Surely it's possible to live this way, to be simply the best of friends, he on his star and she on hers, having fun together when loneliness breathes too heavily down their necks? Surely it's possible?

On Christmas Eve morning, I crept out to the cowshed without waking her. I sang the Christmasy bits of Handel's *Messiah* for the cows, the tenor part. It's the only part I know, but it didn't sound bad.

Then I thought I'd surprise her with Christmas rice pudding in bed, but well, I never! She'd woken up and naturally sneaked a look in the carrier bag of stuff I'd slipped off and bought while she was going on about potash and washed butter. I'd got a plastic sausage of heat-and-serve rice pudding, a tin of gingersnaps and a pack of frozen, ready-cooked ling (she'd been looking for the raw ingredients, dried ling and slaked lime to soak it in). She'd heated some rice pudding in the microwave and set the table with the spindly hyacinths and red candles.

"I'm well aware you don't trust my cooking skills!" she said. "But I'll take photos of your doughnut twists and use them against you if I hear a single word of complaint. You should be damn grateful you're not getting chickpea stew tonight!"

We wrapped ourselves up against the cold and trudged off to cut a tree. We couldn't agree, of course. I wanted to take one of the bent little specimens that would never make good timber, and she wanted a Disney Christmas tree. In the end we found one so ugly she felt sorry for it and wanted to take it home, so we were both happy.

But I couldn't for the life of me find the tree decorations. Mum told me so many important things, but she never revealed where those were kept. So we had to make them ourselves: garlands of kitchen foil; baubles that were my old table tennis balls decorated with colored strips cut from the supermarket Christmas offers leaflet and pictures from the agricultural supplies catalogue. Then we fixed stumps of candles onto the branches with rubber bands and topped it all off with a Toronto maple leaf flag.

"See! Education comes in handy in all sorts of situations," she said, sneaking a cautious glance in my direction. We hadn't mentioned the Big Outburst. "Sunday school!" she said, indicating her garlands. "But what would you have hung them on, if I hadn't had a forest of my own?" I snorted. And neither of us needed to say any more on the subject.

Then we had our Christmas lunch. The Herring à la Russe looked like fresh garden compost, but it tasted great, and so did the mock goose. We put the doughnut twists out for Father Christmas, but on second thought took them in again and threw them straight in the bin. If our house elf had tasted them, he'd probably have set fire to the cowshed. Then we threw away the boiled ling as well; neither of us had ever really liked it, traditional or not.

It turned out she knew the alto part of highlights from the *Messiah*, and we wondered where we could get hold of a soprano. "S'pose we'll have to get together and make one," I said, and then rushed out to the cowshed before I had time to see her face. That was overstepping the mark, I knew. We were supposed to be taking each day as it came; that was our unspoken agreement. I'd have to watch myself.

After evening milking we put our parcels under the tree and tried to wheedle each other into opening one first. We started with harmless, silly presents: I gave her some plastic dog poo to brighten up her antiseptic apartment; she gave me a gangster hat and a tiepin with a dollar sign on it, to wear when I was with my big financier friends. Then she opened a huge pair of hairy wool gloves from me, and I found I had a game called The Haunted Castle. Naturally, neither of us had chosen any presents that so much as hinted at life together; that was all part of our unspoken agreement— but I made so bold as to give her a special present. I'd managed to prise Auntie Astrid out of her silver frame and put in a school photo of me in Year 9.

"It's not really me, but he's the one you like, after all," I said. She blushed a bit.

"And here's something that isn't really you, either, but I hope you might like it," she said. It was a huge tome, a collection of poems by Gunnar Ekelöf. "The natural world replete with love and death around me . . ." she read, looking at me out of the corner of her eye. I resisted making a silly joke about it being just the right size to wedge under the wonky leg of the dining table. She knows very well I kick out like a cross cow whenever she tries to lead me up the cultural path, but I sensed that with this she was trying

142

to give me something that was her, and I thought I'd take a look at it in bed, those evenings I was alone. It couldn't do any harm. Well, I suppose it could, if you dozed off and it fell on your head . . . Oh shut up, Benny!

I kissed her and then we had a game of Haunted Castle. Because the idea was for us to enjoy ourselves, we two lost children in the forest. On Christmas Eve!

The aim of the game was for the players to find their way through a series of rooms, getting past all the obstacles, then steal the treasure and be out before the clock struck midnight. I fell foul of swords, monsters, bottomless pits, and poisonous spiders, but also managed to find secret passages and magic potions. She kept drawing the "Empty Room" card and proceeded primly, square by square. And I was the only one who got out alive, though without any treasure.

Then she started sniveling. Uncertainly, I said, "What a bad loser! Okay, I'll go back in again and fall into the bottomless pit with you."

"It's not that," she said sadly. "But this is the story of my life. Empty rooms."

＋▥＋▥＋▥＋▥ ＋▥＋▥＋▥＋▥＋▥＋▥＋▥＋▥ ＋▥＋▥＋▥＋▥＋▥

Then one day we'll wake, as winter fades away
and skinny, chilled, and matted, look out on the day;
drink in scents of spring like wine in the glade
and search for the honey the wild bees have made.

Regain our strength slowly, roam free in our forest once more;
catch fish in the stream and be glad of the thaw.
Surviving winter, helping each other keep all the warmth in;
we know we'll soon be seeing another spring begin.

Somehow, we both seemed to agree not to let the world
around us get in that Christmas. We didn't leave the farm or
answer the phone. Once, we put out the light in the kitchen
when we saw car headlights coming along the road, then sat
silently holding each other as someone knocked a couple of
times on the door. It was as if we sensed that if we opened
so much as a tiny crack onto the outside world, all manner
of ghouls and ghosts would be blown in and skeletons
would come toppling out of the cupboards.

And I suppose that was what did happen, in the end.

The first ghouls to arrive were Benny's friend Bengt-

Göran and his girl Violet. They were so bloody devious that they came just when they knew Benny would be in the milking parlor and couldn't hide. He brought them in with him and left them to me while he had his shower.

And it went badly from the word go.

Violet had brought a whole bagful of leftovers from their Christmas buffet, which had clearly beaten the one at the best hotel in town by several platter lengths. "Well, Benny told me you didn't really go in for cooking!" she giggled, with a knowing look at the plastic sausage of rice pudding we'd just been scraping out.

I was furious with Benny, of course. I felt betrayed and slandered. And the worst of it was, we'd absolutely nothing left to offer them except a couple of bits of toffee on a plate—and I could hardly start boasting about the mock goose we'd eaten up. Violet started laying out a feast, helping herself from the china cupboard as if she were in her own home. The whole time she was going on about how many different kinds of pickled herring she'd done this year. "Just think, they might give you a whole-page spread in the *Farmer* next year!" I said, and she can't have missed the spiteful tone.

Bengt-Göran seemed to have had quite a few; he said nothing, but stood staring at me with a sickly smile, licking his bottom lip. And the more he licked, the blacker the looks he got from Violet.

So when Benny came upstairs from the cellar, pink from his shower and wearing an innocent smile, the fumes of loathing were already thick in the kitchen air. He did a double take in the doorway, and plainly thought he should make an effort to clear the atmosphere.

"Oh, Violet, what a treasure you are, bringing us some

of your wonderful grub! I've told Desirée all about your smashing meatballs, haven't I, Desirée?"

If only he hadn't mentioned the meatballs! Wound up as I was, I took it as a dig at the ready-made ones I once bought and gave him as an offering.

"Everyone gets the meatballs they deserve!" I said in a dark and mournful tone, and they all stared at me in surprise.

Bengt-Göran gave a sudden snigger, and clearly thought I'd been at the bottle, too. He got out a hip flask and waved it invitingly in my direction. Violet made a great show of turning her solid back on me, and retrieved a gratin dish from the microwave, where she'd put something to heat through. Benny didn't know what was going on and shifted his weight miserably from one foot to another. Traitor!

We sat around the table. Benny ate as if he'd been starved since last Christmas, and joked about my threat to give him chickpea stew. Violet shook her head in sympathy and Bengt-Göran kept trying to refill my wine glass. When I put my hand over the glass, he poured the wine regardless, and offered to lick my hand dry for me. I sharply withdrew the hand, without a word. Benny embarked on a rambling account of his abortive attempt to get the doughnut twists the right shape, and Violet's eyes opened wide: "You mean you were doing the baking . . . ?" she began.

Just then, the telephone rang. I rushed out to the hall.

It was the regional hospital.

"Desirée Wallin? We have a patient here who gave me this number. She'd like you to come and see her if at all possible. You needn't wait for visiting time. Ward 34, room F, it's a single room. But we'd be grateful if you had a word with the duty doctor on your way in. I'm afraid we're not allowed to give details of her condition over the phone. Her name? Oh, didn't I say? It's Märta Oscarsson. She was admitted the day before yesterday. Can I tell her you're coming?"

"Yes, I'm on my way!" I whispered, and went back to the kitchen.

"Can I borrow your car, Benny? Märta's been taken ill!"

I don't know if they believed me, and I couldn't have cared less. I took Benny's truck and went.

"Well, I shan't say a word!" Violet said when Desirée left, and of course, I could hear every word she wasn't saying: What sort of behavior is that, upping and leaving when you've got guests?—who've even taken the trouble to bring something nice to eat, into the bargain.

Because they'd realized she was one of those people who can't even make meatballs! Or won't . . .

Bengt-Göran had had quite a skinful and was mumbling something along the lines of: You'll have to show that one who's boss, all right. Make sure she knows the score. Be tough, they like that. Maybe she's lying there at home right now, waiting for you to come and give her one?

He licked his lips and nudged Violet in the ribs, almost knocking her off her chair. Then they went home with their arms wrapped around each other, and I guess Violet was the only one who got any pleasure out of the whole thing. It's pretty hard to get Bengt-Göran going; she usually starts taunting him about it after his third glass of wine.

Once they'd gone, I just sat there with my hands dangling between my knees, feeling totally at a loss. Why had she gone off like that? Had somebody really been taken ill? Now I know a little of Bengt-Göran and Violet goes a long way, but to be fair, Desirée had introduced me to a few people she knew in town who'd really given me the creeps. It was at the pub, after we'd been to the pictures.

Not that they weren't pleasant, oh no! They were so bloody pleasant to the poor country peasant, kept things nice and simple for him, and instantly translated every four-syllable word that happened to escape their lips into a two-syllable one. Some guy who worked at the higher education college and drove a BMW slapped me on the back and said he'd always wanted to do a physical job, and then, of course, there were all those subsidies and tax breaks, and had I got any decent meat I could sell him? And a prissy little librarian person asked me what farmers did in winter. "You mean while the dairy herd's hibernating?" I retorted, and after that there was a rather strained atmosphere around the table.

I get so fed up listening to people like that. They've read a few indignant articles in the papers about landowners in the south of Sweden getting subsidies, and then they know everything about those crafty farmers who're the big winners in this recession we're having. "So how do you explain the fact that there are loads of farmers going bankrupt every day?" you croak. "In twenty years' time there'll be scarcely a single Swedish farmer left!" But by then, they've started talking about something else.

They ought to declare us a protected species. We're on the verge of extinction, like peregrine falcons and blue anemones. And I know why. I wish I had a chance to tell them that Dad could take the little tractor and chug down to the kiosk and buy a chocolate bar for his profit on a liter of milk. But I'd have to get on the same old tractor, held together with insulation tape and plastic padding, and fork out the whole of my profit on five liters. I don't get much more for my milk than he did twenty years ago, but the price of chocolate hasn't stood still. Or diesel.

And it's a long time since I've been able to afford any relief. Wonder if that BMW guy who liked physical labor would like it quite so much if he had a ninety-hour week, and no extra pay even for working over Christmas?

The worst of it is, you can never say a word to explain it all to those people, even if you knew where on earth to start. Because they'd only exchange knowing looks and oh yeah, those farmers are always moaning. Either there's too much rain for their potatoes, or not enough, ha ha!

Desirée and I have never discussed it, not since the Big Outburst when she got hold of my school grades. She daren't ask me why I don't give it up, though I'm sure she'd like to. And I can't face trying to explain. If I gave up, I'd have to move away from the farm with nothing but old debts to take with me—yes, I won't easily be rid of them; I was so stupid once, I took a million kronor loan for modernization, more money than I'd get if I sold the whole damn junkheap today. And who's to say I'd ever get a job so I could pay the interest on my debts, even? Oh, but you could live in a hostel and get tips on clearing your debts from the Citizens' Advice Bureau . . . not bloody likely!

And if I sell out, if I'm not Benny of Rowan Farm any longer, who am I then?

I'm supposed to have diesel grease under my fingernails and a decent machinery store with gas welding gear and pressure cleaning equipment; I'm supposed to subscribe to *Animal Husbandry* and *Farmers' Journal Exchange and Mart*; I'm supposed to have two tractors, a John Deere and a Valmet, plus a round baler, a manure spreader, and a forestry hoist! Until the Senior Enforcement Officer forces me into an insolvency auction.

If you take my John Deere away and put me in a suit, I shall feel like a transvestite.

But we've just skirted around the margins of the topic, Desirée and I. She once asked me if there was anything else except cows a farmer could make a profit out of; I suppose she was thinking of carp farming or everlasting flowers or something. I answered curtly that the only profitable trades in the world these days seemed to involve arms, drugs, and sex.

So then we started sketching out a plan to convert the farm to an original sort of sex club. Desirée wanted to call it Kinky Country Club: Roll Up and See How Animals Do It! Does rubber gear turn you on? Then come and see the inseminator in boots and rubber apron fertilize a cow! Book a space in the hayloft for a nostalgic Silver Wedding night! Pep up your sex life with a bit of S&M: hire a cow bridle and tether each other! Or try a Rowan Farm Special, a sex kick you'll never forget! Get it on against our electric fence . . .

It's getting pretty well worn now, that path we always divert onto when any question that might possibly be important seems to be coming to a head. We come up with a joke and skirt around anything that could prove awkward.

Where the hell has she got to?

All the spilled milk you wiped up for me;
all the laughs with which you rubbed me warm.
There's nothing I can give you in return.
Your windows are dark and the key is gone.

I'd seen Märta on the 23rd, and then she was looking like something out of a picture book—cheeks rosy, eyes gleaming, her arms full of sparkly parcels.

Now, sitting on a red plastic chair in the psychiatric unit, I found a distinctly middle-aged woman with a pale, puffy face, and empty hands resting on her knees, palms uppermost. I knelt down in front of her and put my arms around her; she rested her chin on my shoulder and I could sense she was staring straight ahead at the opposite wall.

For a long time we said nothing.

"What did he do?" I asked in the end. I simply couldn't imagine what it could be; Robert had put her through so much already, and she'd always bounced back.

She didn't answer. More time passed, then her eyes focused again and she asked, with a discontented frown:

"Why bother living? So pointless and tiresome!" She stared at me accusingly.

I couldn't think of anything helpful to say, when the question was put like that.

"But you did want me to come," I faltered.

"Me?" she said. "I don't want anything!"

I went to visit her every day, sitting silently beside her for hours. It didn't seem to disturb her, at any rate. If I asked how she was feeling, she'd mumble things like "All the indicators have sunk into the red zone and the last krona has fallen out through a hole in my pocket."

On the fourth day, her face pulled itself into a crooked smile and she told me about a test they'd made her fill in, to find out whether she was suicidal. Page after page, hundreds of questions like: "Do you find life meaningless? Always/often/sometimes" and "Do you feel worthless? Constantly/usually/often."

"If you weren't suicidal before the test, you definitely would be by the end!" she said, showing a glimpse of her old self. And then she told me.

Six months before, Robert had talked her into agreeing to be sterilized. She wasn't able to use a coil and Robert found anything else too off-putting. She thought about it for a long time before swallowing, like a bitter pill, the fact that Robert didn't want to pay maintenance for any more children. She wanted Robert, and everything has its price.

The evening before Christmas Eve, a woman rang and asked to speak to Robert. When he hung up, he mumbled something, put on his leather jacket, and went out.

He didn't come back. Märta spent Christmas Eve alone. But she knew Robert, knew better than to ring the police or worry about traffic accidents. She would find out in due course, and she was already bracing herself for the blow.

He turned up on the 27th, hand in hand with a young girl whom Märta at first thought sad and dumpy.

Then she saw that the girl must be five months pregnant, if not more.

It transpired that Robert had finally found True Love for the first time, and wanted to do everything he could for Jeanette and the baby. They were on their way to parenting classes at the maternity clinic, and could he borrow Märta's car over New Year, since they were old friends? Jeanette had family outside town.

He addressed Märta, whose partner he'd been—on and off—for twelve years, with vaguely distracted affection, as if she were a cousin or an old school friend.

"And that was the way he saw it, just then. I'd swear to it!" Märta said.

"Haven't you got enough kids already?" was all she said to Robert.

"Well, you wouldn't understand, would you, Märta?" Robert answered without turning a hair. "I mean, you've deliberately chosen not to have any children in your life. You can't understand how much a man can long for children when he's found the right woman."

Märta lent them the car. Just to get them out of the apartment, double quick.

My hands were shaking when I got back to the library.

A week later, Märta was discharged. She stood in my kitchen, chopping onions for lunch.

"I feel like an extra in the film of my own life," she said. "I'm milling around in the background and charging in and out with armies and mobs and saying rhubarb rhubarb in

154

crowds. But there's someone else in close-up in the fore-ground. It's just that I can't see who it is."

She often expressed herself in dreamlike terms now, without embarrassment or explanation. And then she did something that really moved me.

She happened to cut her thumb with the knife, a deep gash. She stared at the blood for a few moments, then caught sight of the ridiculous poster Benny had bought me of the couple in the shell.

She padded quickly across the room, climbed onto the sofa and pressed her thumb over the woman's eyes, gentle as a caress.

Now the woman in the shell was crying blood.

She couldn't even drive my car back to the farm, because she had to sit with her friend at the hospital, she said. She sat there all day long and worked evenings. I had to take the bus in and fetch the car from town; she'd perched the keys on one of the tires. The car was parked outside her block of apartments. I went into the courtyard and stared up at her window. Her blinds were down—those slatted wooden ones; she hadn't got any proper curtains.

She wasn't answering the phone, hadn't even left the answering machine on.

Five days went by and I heard nothing from her. I made a start on all the official forms about the farm that came shooting out of my mailbox every blessed day. If she ever comes here again, she'll find my cold corpse suffocated by an avalanche of forms, I thought. And then I expect she'll put me under one of those surveyor's marker stones and start looking around for the next poor devil on a bench in the cemetery. I was trying really hard to be mad at her; it hurt a bit less that way, and at least I could get some sleep.

I mean, I didn't know if she just didn't give a shit about me or if she really had a good reason for staying away. Would I have done the same for Bengt-Göran? Sat with him day after day in the psychiatric ward, taken time off work and made it up in the evenings? Had no time to ring her?

Huh, there's no way I can picture myself doing that! Blimey, there's nothing in Bengt-Göran's head to go wrong. You could lobotomize him with the power saw and nobody would notice the difference. And we're not that sort of mates; it's more a case of a habit we've had since we were kids, and I haven't had time to find anyone else.

And at the back of my mind I was as suspicious of "nerves" as a lot of the older folk around here. "They should have shot the first psychologist, then we wouldn't have had any problems," one old chap said. Those weren't real illnesses. Only shirkers blamed their nerves, to avoid pulling their weight.

If I'd gone on like that when Shrimp was there, she'd have felled me onto the couch with a kick to the groin, analyzed me into small bits, and put me back together again, I know that all right.

Then all of a sudden, she rang. She sounded stressed and my ears pricked up. "What is it?"

"It's heavy going at the moment," was all she said. I wondered if she was going to dump me there and then, over the phone. Think quickly, Benny.

"I shall be thirty-seven on Friday," I blurted out, before she could interrupt. "Do you want to go out somewhere with me? I know you're hardly in the mood for champagne, but a swift beer or something? It's not an important day or anything." Nervous as hell.

"Or a teeny-weeny glass of low-alcohol cider on such a totally insignificant day?" She sounded a bit more cheerful, and then she said she'd organize the celebrations and come over the night before so she could bring me breakfast in bed. I warbled with delight like some bloody skylark. She was coming back!

There've been times when I've sat on my cemetery bench and wondered if the beginning of the end was when Violet and Bengt-Göran lugged their movable feast through the door, or whether it happened on my birthday. I mean, we were still together, Shrimp and I—it was more as if the oxygen was starting to run out.

It all started so well. The evening before my birthday, we fooled around and giggled just like in the good old days, and had some generous prebirthday samples from the bottle of dry champagne she'd brought, which I honestly thought tasted like something fermented in my can of formic acid. She rummaged and banged about behind the closed kitchen door, and hid something in my wardrobe. I clung onto her that night as if I were a drowning man, and she the only life raft in sight. It was late when we got to sleep.

In the morning, the alarm clock woke me as usual. I stole a glance in her direction, waiting for my coffee.

But she was still asleep! I lay there for a bit, chewing my nails and wondering if I could discreetly make her wake up. I set the alarm off again and cleared my throat like some old consumptive. But she didn't stir. Probably something to do with the fact that she usually starts work at ten, while I start at six.

I got out to the cowshed half an hour later than my usual milking time, with very mixed feelings and suffering the aftereffects of yesterday's sour champagne. And nothing went to plan. Because I was late, the cows were more unruly than usual and a heifer kicked me on the shin. I wasn't in the best of moods by the time I'd finished.

When I got in, I showered as fast as I could and then opened the kitchen door a crack to peep in. The place was deserted. She hadn't woken up.

Hell, I was glad she was there, anyway, in the same house. It was uncalled for, really, to go up to the bedroom and get dressed as noisily as I could to see how she reacted.

"Do I catch a whiff of burning martyr?" I heard from the tangle of bedclothes. She looked at the clock and peered at me through half-shut eyes.

"I wasn't expecting anything," I mumbled.

"What's that supposed to mean?"

Angry, pale blue eyes, white eyelashes blinking in irritation. She jumped up and started pulling on her marvelous underwear, one-hundred-percent unbleached cotton. "Well then, you'll get exactly what you expected. Nothing!"

Was it my fault now? Without a word, I lumbered downstairs; she followed, managing to stamp angrily even in stockinged feet.

I turned on the tap to fill the coffee pot. The tap exploded and spat air. Damn it! The bloody pump had broken down again! I'd have to go out and look. And get hold of a plumber!

Shrimp gave me a surreptitious glance as she fussed about with something in the fridge.

"There won't be any coffee!" I said. "The pump's stopped again!"

"Then we'll have beer and cake!" she smiled. But I was too worked up to note the softening of her tone. It didn't occur to her that when the water runs out on a farm, not being able to make coffee's a minor matter. Your main problem is twenty-four thirsty cows, plus followers.

"Beer! Swedish cows don't drink beer, even if I did happen to have a few hundred liters on hand! But it's a good job you're here: I need an assistant. I'll have a go at fixing it myself before I ring the plumber! We'll have to get out there right away," I said, trying to sound a bit friendlier.

She looked at me and didn't budge from the spot. I'd already got my jacket on. "Take this!" I said, throwing her my leather one. "And you can get Mum's boots—they're in the wardrobe. What are you waiting for?"

"Nothing!" she hissed. "I've got a job waiting for me! You'll have to find somebody else to be your farmhand today!"

There was nothing more to be said. I ran to the pump shed, and after a while, I heard her car start, over by the house.

I struggled with the pump on my own for a couple of hours, fueled by pure rage, but it was a job that needed two people. I got absolutely nowhere, and went in to ring the plumber. On the kitchen table was something that looked like an enormous pork sausage, and a cow pie on a plate. Turned out to be a whole roll of salt beef, plus a very odd-looking chocolate cake. There was a note beside them.

"Benny! You're an idiot, and so am I. Eat the cake, sweat

and toil all day, then come around to my place by half past six this evening. Leave your overalls at home—I'm taking you out to celebrate."

I was too exhausted to feel anything. The main thought in my mind was that if I collapsed on the settee, I might get a couple of hours' sleep. I ate a bit of the cake and salt beef, lay down on the kitchen banquette and had just dozed off when the plumber tooted his horn in the yard. Out again, tired as hell. It took several hours to fix the pump, and then it was milking time again.

At half past six I threw myself into the car, smartly turned out, my hair slicked down with water. The chocolate cake and the salt beef were fighting it out in my guts; I hadn't had time to eat anything else. I hope she takes me to some really blood-oozing steakhouse, I thought. Béarnaise sauce!

Lack of sleep and food is the best explanation I have for what happened later that evening.

Enchanted gold is what I offered you.
It turned back to dead leaves in the sun
and you looked in bafflement at my eager face.

It wasn't that I'd forgotten Benny, those days I spent sitting with Märta at the hospital. I'd just put him on hold, because I could only cope with one thing at a time.

Several times I was on the verge of pouring out the whole story to Märta—for years I've been the sort who tries to talk through anything I can't get to grips with by myself. But I couldn't do that on this occasion. And whenever I thought of goddamned Robertino, I just wanted to hang all men up by their thumbs. Reality somehow stopped during those days. All I did was sit, work, and sleep. And brooded. Depression's contagious; don't let anybody tell you otherwise.

In the end I rang him. And I was roused from my gloomy torpor as I heard him say it was his birthday and remembered what he'd done for me on mine. I went out to the shops and bought champagne and roses and a whole roll of salt beef, which he loves. Then, after much thought, I went to the workwear shop and bought myself a set of overalls; he was supposed to realize it was actually intended as a present to him. Yes, I'd toddle out and help him sometimes, to show my Solidarity as best I could. And I bought two tickets for *Rigoletto*: there was a touring production in town. It's my very favorite opera—no one can resist it. Or so I thought. And I suppose I thought of it as some kind of tit-for-tat, the overalls for the opera.

I smuggled the overalls into his wardrobe and made a quick chocolate cake from a mix. All I can say is, it didn't turn out at all like the picture on the packet. I was planning to appear at his bedside in the overalls, with coffee and cake, singing and waving the tickets. I put the roses out on the porch to keep them fresh. Then we curled up on the sofa, wrapped fetuslike around each other, the champagne between us. That night was glorious: I felt like his Siamese twin. I didn't know you could get that close to somebody without actually sharing the same blood circulation system.

And then I overslept.

That was bad enough. I felt so ashamed of myself, as soon as I realized where I was. Benny was clomping around the bedroom, keeping his back turned, and on that back, spelled out in big letters, was the message: It's my Birthday, but I've got to Work and Toil while Others Enjoy a Lie-in! And in smaller letters: I didn't even get my coffee!

"I wasn't expecting anything from you, anyhow," he said, and I suddenly saw red. I couldn't cope with being a Siamese twin one minute and all this shame and guilt the next. I snapped at him that he certainly wouldn't be getting anything from me, and I meant the overalls, my acknowledgment of his work, and my help, such as it was.

Later, in the kitchen, I'd calmed down enough to want to give him the cake. But he was suddenly standing over me clutching a leather jacket and ordering me out to work, snorting something about cows not drinking beer, just to make me feel even more useless.

Once he'd gone, I threw the overalls in the car, chucked away the roses, which had naturally frozen overnight, and sat down at the kitchen table, breathing heavily. In the end I wrote him a note. It had all gone so pathetically wrong; I had to do something.

He didn't turn up until quarter past seven that evening, with wet hair and a cautious smile. I had thought I'd explain a few things over a bite to eat before the performance, to put us in a positive mood for drinking in *Rigoletto*, but we never got time. We rushed to the theater and I just had time to say "Happy Birthday" before the overture began. He nodded, and peered at the program in the gloom.

I don't love all opera; the plot of *Die Fledermaus*, for example, seems so silly to me that I can hardly see the point of sitting through it. I'd rather listen to it on CD. But *Rigoletto*: now there's an opera with blood and guts, all about guilt and innocence and love against all better judgment, and with music to lift you through the roof. For me that evening, Gilda and her doomed passion stood for Märta, sitting there mutely in her hospital ward. In the closing scene, when Gilda gives her life for the Duke as he's laughing with a new woman, I couldn't control my tears. I was much occupied with my handkerchief as the lights went up, and hoped Benny would understand.

But I needn't have worried. He was fast asleep. He'd turned a little to one side and was snoring in an unlovely fashion, with his chin resting on the edge of his seat and his mouth open. It took me ten minutes to wake him properly, and everybody was staring at us.

That was the rest of the evening spoiled. We didn't say a word to each other as we walked back to his car, I didn't even ask him to spend the night. He had to get up at six as usual.

Back at the car, he touched my cheek with his maimed hand and gave a wan smile.

"Are we quits?" he asked. And I couldn't help kissing his knuckles.

It's obvious it won't work. Not a cat in hell's chance.

It's not only the farm. I can just picture myself coming in at night completely shattered—after haymaking, say—and there she is waiting with the opera tickets, drumming her fingers. Opera, good grief! All through the first act, I felt as if my stomach was rumbling louder than that fatso with the sword, who was howling fit to call the cows home. Shrimp should be grateful I fell asleep; I'd have shown her up even worse if I'd been conscious. I might even have said what I really thought—out loud.

But she wasn't very happy. I could see that, all right.

We scarcely see eye to eye on anything. We take care to avoid politics these days. I remember the first confrontation. It started with me showing her a letter to the paper that I thought was great; it ended with her calling me a fascist and going to sleep with her back to me. And there've been other times. These days we avert our eyes uncomfortably when anything crops up on television that we know we'll disagree about.

I suppose we were born under incompatible star signs. That's what Auntie Astrid would have said; she was very keen on all that business. Mum and I used to tease her when she got all serious about what we ought to do while the ascendant was in Jupiter. I came across a newspaper article that claimed all our modern horoscopes are a month out, because the Roman calendar they used when the system was first set up has shifted over the centuries. Auntie Astrid was so confused we felt sorry for her. She'd identified so totally with the role of a handsome, good-hearted ox, and now it turned out she was a fish.

Shrimp reads horoscopes as well, but mostly just to wind me up. "If you'd been born two days earlier, you'd have been a dreamy, artistic type who enjoys life and takes each day as it comes," she said pointedly once, reading the horoscope sign before mine. Hanging in the air was the implication that things would have been much easier that way. "Dreamy dairy farmers who take each day as it comes go broke or get run over by their tractor," I muttered.

But our horoscopes may be the only thing that can explain why we feel attracted to each other in spite of the fact we're both kicking out against it—because I think we are, now. They ought to get some old fortune-teller to look into it. Maybe it's some bloody transcendent in Venus that's in the twelfth house of Mars? Isn't there any chance of bending those lines and circles and getting free at least, so I can stop dreaming about pale little shrimps and stride off into the sunset with a muscular, domesticated young woman from the farmers' relief service? And Shrimp could settle down with some weirdy beardy with long summer holidays and eighteen meters of bookshelves.

We've carried on seeing each other since the disastrous birthday, but it's as if we're always on our guard with each other, exaggerating the impossibility of it all. "I can't take any time off in the summer, but if I could take a couple of days in September, I fancy the Lofoten Islands. For the fishing!" I say brightly. "That wouldn't be your sort of thing at all, would it?"

"Oh no! I'd prefer the avant-garde theater festival in Avignon. In July!" she retorts, adding, "They perform in French, you know."

We're trying to convince each other and ourselves that we should leave the party while we're still having fun. Before it ends in tears. Hurting Shrimp is the last thing I want to do; I'd rather chop off the fingers I've got left.

I don't think she realizes that. I hate it, for example, when she starts listing all the atrocious things Robert's done to her friend Märta. She often does that, these days. Every time she starts, I feel she's somehow accusing me; I don't think she realizes she's got that "men are all the same" tone of voice. Sometimes I say things like, "Well, what the hell, maybe she provoked him!" and that makes her blow her top. "But I'm not like that," I'll say. "You think we're all selfish and prey on women—but just because I'm a guy, it doesn't mean I should take the blame for what other men do! Do you take responsibility for all the whites' dirty tricks on other races, eh? Because you certainly are white!"

Then she says she's never claimed I'm Robert and why should I feel the need to defend him? At least he didn't subject Märta to physical abuse, she adds—and there I am, left with the shame again, the shame of all those men who batter their women. We never get anywhere.

And after those run-ins, the place is like a minefield strewn with everything we've said and not yet said, and it's difficult to play our games. Playing used to be our forte, when we first started.

But if I'm brutally honest with myself, that's not my main problem. No, it's something else that's been brought home to me very clearly since Mum died.

What I want and need is a woman who can put together some kind of a home. It doesn't matter if she buys the meatballs and uses cake mixes; she can even put up curtains made of sticks and buy clothes that look as if the council handed them out—as long as she cares and gets some sort of system going, so a man feels at home. You can buy your own meatballs, Shrimp would say; and I've got clothes enough to cover my body—but it's always as if I'm only managing the very basics: taking nourishment to survive; clothing myself to avoid arrest by the police.

Soon I won't need to worry about losing the farm and ending up in a hostel for homeless men. It's bloody well starting to look like a hostel here already. And I haven't a clue how to turn it into a home. I think I could manage without sex; after all, I've had to, over long periods. But being homeless on your own farm is no fun at all.

And I don't think Shrimp wants to make a home. Or knows how to.

I haven't even a stick to light a fire,
just a handful of bent drawing pins
and a pair of pliers

Life was increasingly falling into two halves. Inez Lundmark had taken early retirement, which meant I was in sole charge of the Children's section. I buried myself totally in my work: planned a children's theater week; got local artists in to do story illustrations with the children; started trying to put pressure on local politicians to invest more in cultural projects—usually with the result that some political party claimed me as its own. I reckon I was gaining a nice little reputation as a person with a lot of ideas who got things done. I attended book fairs and courses, and almost persuaded a big boss at the council to finance a children's film festival. But it turned out not to be the festival itself that interested him. He suggested we make a joint visit to a children's film festival in Poland one weekend. His secretary rang me to ask if it was correct that we wanted a double room, and all the affectionate hugs and "darlings" suddenly fell into place. When I confronted him, his first excuse was that he'd wanted to save the council money . . . and we were modern people, weren't we? Then he said his secretary had misunderstood and was an incompetent who might soon find herself superfluous to requirements. And then there was no children's film festival.

I couldn't see any way of taking it further; it would just have created problems for the secretary. They generally make sure they hedge their bets and protect their backs, men like that. But I'm not sure his aims were limited to a little adventure within the snug confines of the council hierarchy—sometimes he'd ring at nights and sniffle and slur down the phone. I told Benny, and he offered to put on a false moustache and go undercover at the council offices. That was one of the few times I succeeded in interesting him in what I did—I think he was a bit jealous.

The worst thing wasn't the unwanted attentions of this council bigwig, or the fact that the film festival came to nothing. Experience has taught me to go easy when I'm trying to be nice to men; some of them seem to have an incomprehensible weakness for women like me. They initially assume I'm all feeble and fragile, and when it dawns on them that I might not be, they feel a need to make it their personal mission to solve the puzzle. It's happened before.

No, the worst thing was that this bigwig's wife is a library colleague of mine. She didn't know anything about it, of course—after all, there wasn't much to know—but I'd hear her in the staff room, as I had done for years: "Now the children have flown the nest, Sten and I have finally got more time for each other! If only Sten could take some time off, we'd go to Madeira for our anniversary, a second honeymoon! Sten and I and Sten and I . . ."

And at nights I had Sten sniveling on the phone.

We seemed to have a lot of husbands in the staff room for a while. Lilian mostly complained about hers: ". . . and when I get home from work after being on my feet for ten hours, he's just sitting there at the kitchen table with the evening paper spread out over the empty eggshells and cornflake bowls from breakfast, asking what's for dinner. And he always needs consoling about something or other: because he didn't win the lottery, or because somebody at work's been annoying him, or because he's going bald. The most restful times are actually when he's ill, because then he just lies in his room groaning, and the kids and I can do what we like for a change . . ."

". . . Just think! Sten would never do anything like that! He's so considerate he often has breakfast at work . . ."

They went on in that vein and got seriously on my nerves. Because I was pretty sure they once felt for their husbands something of what was currently attracting me to Benny. I mean, I'm too old to believe the "We'll never get like that" line, especially as things are already less than rosy.

So life fell into two halves: the enjoyable, hard work that kept me busy by day—and the time outside that, which I increasingly devoted to turning things over in my mind.

Sten. Lilian's husband. Robertino. And Örjan.

And Benny?

How high a price was I prepared to pay, and what did I really want?

There was really only one person I could ask. So I went around to her place.

We're seeing less and less of each other.

She can't borrow her friend's car any more; the friend seems to have got rid of it, so either I have to go and fetch her or she has to catch a bus. There's only one, at 7:30 on weekdays. That means she's here at half past eight, and by ten I should be getting to bed. And I can rarely pick her up before about eight, so it gets just as late. If I sleep over at her place, I have to get up at five.

An hour and a half, once or twice a week. Not counting the weeks she's away.

When what we need is a clear run of a couple of days to get under the jokey surface. I mean, you can't just come out with "Have we got any future together?" when she's standing in the hall, hanging up her coat.

I forgot the weekends. Then she's here for a whole day sometimes. That's when we quarrel. Or avoid quarreling, which is almost as exhausting.

But I miss them, all the same—she's been away at conferences and courses and all sorts of other nonsense these last three weekends. Damned if I won't have to start seeing her at the cemetery again.

I took her to a party, here in the village. It was a kind of experiment, I suppose. Things were a bit frosty between her and Violet, but the other villagers, most of them over fifty, seemed to take to her. She was talking to some of them so eagerly that I started worrying she was suggesting books for them to read, but apparently they were talking about village history. Genuine interest on both sides can never do any harm—and what's more, I know my neighbors are quite touchingly concerned to see me safely settled. The way we see it, when the last farm goes, the village dies—we all feel that way, deep down. It becomes just another outlying outpost of the town.

I remember sitting there glumly over my beer, imagining Rowan Farm as a holiday home for some executive in a computer firm.

Then we were invited around for coffee by Aunt Alma and Uncle Gunnar, Mum's old friends. On the Sunday.

"Oh, I'm afraid I can't! I've got to fly to Uppsala at three tomorrow afternoon!" Desirée said.

What can I say?

On my own in the cowshed, I keep coming back to the thought that there are three ways to go from here, and I'll have to make up my mind soon.

One: I try to get Desirée to uproot herself and move here. She hasn't the least intention of doing that, I know—she'd be annoyed if I even asked.

Two: I sell the farm and move into town and keep the coffee hot for when she gets back from Uppsala. I haven't the least intention of doing that.

And three: I look reality in the eye and give up the whole impossible business. Then I try to find a more suitable woman, who'd be prepared to spend more than three hours a week with me. Because the fourth alternative, which I don't even want to contemplate, is staying a bachelor into old age. Like Bosse, who folk still call Nilssons' lad, though he's forty-six. He's single and lives at his parents' farm with his old mother, keeps a few beef cows, and works half the week at the agricultural supplier's. He's had a huge satellite dish installed, gets envelopes through the post marked "Discretion guaranteed," and lives for capercaillie hunting. He has no other interests, as far as I know. He drops in at Rowan Farm occasionally on some unlikely errand and stays for three hours, and if Desirée happens to be here, we both sigh behind the curtains when we see his car turning into the yard.

No, at all costs avoid getting like Bosse. Söderströms' lad, fifty-three . . . I'd do anything to escape that. And now we're coming to the crunch.

Perhaps Desirée senses a swarm of aging bachelor angst buzzing in the air when she comes to visit me. She's aware of all the expectations and sets her face against them and just wants to be a playmate. Little Shrimp, hardly out of childhood, not afraid of being alone in her busy, urban life.

Whenever—increasingly rarely, now—I get her to myself, in my bed, I feel as if I've got a stone sinking in my belly. Because she's just as dizzyingly white, warm, and graceful as ever, and I tell her: "It's your fault if I die prematurely! Unmarried men have a poor prognosis, you know, statistically speaking!" And as she ties herself in knots with the effort of avoiding giving me an answer, she doesn't realize the bell's ringing for the last act.

+✠+✠+✠+✠+✠+✠+✠+✠+✠+✠+✠+✠+✠+✠+✠+✠+✠

> *I don't want to break the finishing tape,*
> *run fast, throw things—*
> *why should it be more worthwhile to jump over the bar*
> *than go straight under it?*

Naturally, I tried to make it look like a polite social call. I took flowers, expensive tulips, and a packet of the best Darjeeling.

She opened the door but kept the chain on. When she saw who it was, she let me in, though without enthusiasm. She didn't seem averse to my being there, merely distracted. Like someone who's really a bit too busy to have visitors.

"Hello, Inez!" I said. "It's been quite a while! How are things with you?"

"What? That can't be particularly interesting information for you, can it?" she asked, not unkindly.

It seemed to me that Inez now thought life too short for small talk. So I decided there and then not to beat about the bush.

"Well, yes, it is a bit!" I said. "I've been thinking about you a lot. Your way of looking at life, and how wise you must be. I'd like you to let me share a little of it."

"Hmm?" she said noncommittally.

"There must have been a time when you had to make a choice," I said. "Now I've got to make one, too, and soon. It would be interesting to know what your thinking was. How you came to choose your archives rather than firsthand experience. Do you see?"

Two red patches suddenly flared on her cheeks; she got up and put the tulips in an old-fashioned crystal vase she dug out from the back of a kitchen cupboard. I could see her climbing on a chair to reach it. Then she came in and sat down again, took off her glasses, and shot me a look of annoyance.

"What makes you think I had any choice? Of course I didn't have any choice when it came to firsthand experience! My parents were missionaries in Tanzania; I was brought up by an unmarried aunt. She was a terribly messy and disorganized person, incidentally! When I got a place at library school, it came as a huge, intoxicating liberation for me. Being free to organize things the way I wanted. In systems. Of course, I could have chosen to experience things myself. Gone on china-painting courses and group tours. That's never appealed to me in the least! I went on to work at the library for thirty-seven years, voilà tout! And you may as well know that I'm not interested in having 'friends I can confide in.' Do you see?"

"If you throw me out, Inez, I'll go home and open a computer file on you!" I said. That produced a little smile.

Then we talked for nearly an hour. She made us each a cup of my Darjeeling, though the strength she brewed it, it might as well have been a Tetley's teabag.

"What I need from you is a word of advice," I said. "Just an extra pair of eyes. Sharp eyes like yours. What did you mean when you told me that Benny was either totally wrong or the only conceivable one?"

She got up, went over to the filing cabinet and rooted around until she found my file.

"Hm . . . I've only observed you together on three occasions," she said. "The latest one was just after Christmas, before I retired. I don't need to go into how totally wrong he is, I'm sure you're all too aware of it. His clothes . . . and you do choose the way you want to look, consciously or unconsciously. But the other thing. All those feelings I could see. On both sides. Your husband seemed a likeable chap, but you didn't stop work when he came in. You didn't drop things and you didn't pretend not to know him, not even at the very start. You somehow didn't think it worth the bother. But this other one—you were almost rude to him. And then he held onto that book you gave him as tightly as if it were a much-loved puppy. Well, there's not much more I can say, because I've no experience in these matters. But I've seen it before and it never lasts," she added, almost with relish.

"The only conceivable one?" I persisted.

"I said it because you were different. I've never seen you like that before. And now you'll have to excuse me; I've got a lot to do."

She showed me her latest project. She'd started collecting and filing promotion leaflets, sending away for special offers, entering competitions, and keeping a record of the results.

"But I don't like it when they write to me as 'Dear I. Maria Lundmark,'" she said sternly.

Inez knows who she is, and they need to learn that. There's got to be some sense of order to things.

Why the hell does everything have to be so bloody impossible? I thought that one day, when I'd forgotten to check which cows were in heat because I was chatting away on the phone with Shrimp. Two grown-up people about the same age, one house, a town nearby, two jobs. Live together, commute, do up the house . . . have children. Sleep together every night, see each other more than three hours a week.

I could picture it all so vividly that I glossed over all the obstacles we'd run headlong into before. I simply decided it was time for action at my end and started planning some alterations to the house.

The house at Rowan Farm is a pretty big one. A large kitchen, one smaller room, a sitting room, and a big entrance hall. Two bedrooms upstairs and a loft that could be used if I got it insulated. We could make the smaller room downstairs into a workroom for her . . . the only thing in there is Mum's big weaving loom; it seems quite a while since I was last in there. My bedroom for us, Mum's room for the children . . . and no doubt we can squeeze in her bloody bookshelves somehow.

Then I tried to work out whether we'd be able to afford a car for her. If she sells her apartment and hasn't got the repayments to think about . . . realistically, she won't be able to work full-time, and she'll probably take a few years off when the first one's born . . . or do a bit of part-time, if she really wants to. There's no nursery in the village . . . but maybe Violet would do a bit of childminding . . .

I went on like that, and yeah, it gave those last weeks a golden glow, before all hell broke loose with the stress of the summer months. I was so absorbed in my calculations that I completely forgot Shrimp. Then one day—she was in the middle of some theater festival for kids, and rather reluctantly came out by bus—I told her I'd got something important to say. I parked her on the chaise longue, fetched my papers and sketches and calculations, and launched into it.

She didn't ask any questions, didn't say anything at all. The only sound she made was a quiet moan when I got to the bit about part-time work, kids, and Violet child-minding. When I'd finished, there was dead silence for a moment.

Then Desirée said her piece.

She reminded me about that bitch I had, the one who tried to climb the walls, frantic to get out.

I've done my best to try to forget what she said. It was all about how she couldn't see herself—*visualize*, she said—spending the rest of her summers taking picnic baskets to the edge of fields, or on her own in some boardinghouse with any children there happened to be. Said that she loved her job and had had to struggle to get where she was. That she couldn't be in charge of a children's section if she was working half the hours, and a part-time librarian's wage would hardly be enough to run a car—she'd have to ask me for extra if she so much as wanted to go and get her hair cut. And that she'd rather have an abortion than have Violet as her childminder.

By that point, it was all over as far as I was concerned.

She wittered on about how we were jogging along quite nicely as we were and we could always wait and see—and I hadn't the energy to say no.

Then she started talking about the importance of paternity leave and all the places she wanted to go on summer holidays. I didn't even ask her if she'd ever heard of a dairy farmer on paternity leave who was free in the summer. I just sat there nodding, like an old wind-up toy.

She rang the next day and said she realized she'd been a bit harsh; she blamed premenstrual tension. But she was going to come out and bring something really nice for our dinner on Saturday evening.

It was the first time she'd ever done anything like that. Little Shrimp, she can't even see it's all over. And I'm steeling myself to tell her.

✦✖✦✖✦✖✦ ✦✖✦✖ ✖✦✖✦✖ ✦✖✦✖✦✖✦✖✦✖ ✦✖✦✖✦✖✦✖

I could have reeled it in carefully,
bagged it with the net,
cleaned and gutted it,
then enjoyed a good meal—
but it tore itself off the hook:
goddamned love!

Red alert, as the military would say. Keep your rifle
cocked; the enemy's on the prowl out there.

There's been a red alert in my relationship with Benny
for several weeks now. The problem is sighting the enemy.

Something had happened that felt like the beginning of
the end—but when exactly?

Of course, you could claim it happened the first time
we met.

But in fact, I suppose it happened that evening Benny
lined up all his sketches for alterations to the house and his
financial calculations: how I'd sell the apartment that
belonged to Örjan and me and give up my job. Or at least
work part-time.

I felt as if I was suffocating, like some mental asthma

attack. Because here he was, rubbing my nose in reality, the very reality I'd carefully been taking wide detours around. Of course I'd worried about us—but about our "feelings" and how different we were. Whether our "feelings" could take all the strain as we worked on them. Because if they couldn't, the question of where to live was irrelevant.

I suppose I'd vaguely convinced myself he would come around to the view that milk production was all too much effort in the long run, and I was sure he'd be able to get a job with some tractor company—he was so good with engines. And then we'd get a place nearer town. If he was determined to hang onto the family farm, he could always find a tenant for it in the interim. Somewhere at the back of my mind, I knew I was being overoptimistic; after his furious outburst back in the autumn, when I found his final report card, I had my suspicions it wouldn't be that simple. But as I say, I'd successfully managed to keep the question at bay. And here he was, coming up to me, depositing it in my lap and wagging his tail.

When he proposed Violet as a childminder, I couldn't contain myself any longer.

So I told him how I saw things, and I didn't pull any punches. I knew it was operation overkill, but he had to get the message Loud and Clear, once and for all. Even so, I didn't want to burn all my bridges. I said encouraging things about biding our time and letting our relationship deepen, defining our needs and deciding which ones to prioritize so we could adapt to each other. I must have sounded like a marriage guidance counselor bringing her work home with her. I wanted to get him thinking along new lines. Wouldn't he like to travel and see the world with me, for example? Or get really close to his child, take paternity leave, give me a chance to make the most of my career?

He seemed to be taking it all in. He sat nodding thoughtfully, all the way through.

So then you might have expected we'd get started on all that adapting and deepening. But quite the opposite. We buried ourselves back in our lives and neither of us gave an inch of ground.

It got almost competitive. Benny did everything short of spitting snuff on the floor and getting into knife fights to show me he was a simple farming lad, and I assumed the role of Clever and Cultured Career woman. Three Cs, and you could have made it four by adding Completely misguided.

We weren't trying to bridge any gaping chasms; we were trying to hurl each other into them. Maybe we were both hoping for a miracle. I was hoping he'd admit he had a soul, and I expect he was hoping I'd sprout an apron overnight. We made a spirited fight of it, because the power of attraction between us was still so strong we felt we might fall into a black hole at any moment. The other side of the coin was that we argued with each other more bitterly than we'd ever done.

Then we stopped sleeping together. It was too much of a strain. Too painful on the heartstrings.

And there wasn't much left after that.

Because we'd reached a point where we couldn't just be together and have a nice time; we each had to be working on our barricades all the time. It actually ended where it all started: in the cemetery. We went there together one day and tended our graves, side by side.

Suddenly Benny said: "Do you think you and I will ever end up under the same headstone?" He gave me a thoughtful look.

I glanced at his stone and a shiver ran through me. "But which stone? Surely that's the question," I said.

"Because I don't think we ever will!" Benny went on.

It took a moment to sink in. He didn't believe in us any more.

Not now and not ever.

Something inside me started hurting like mad.

I reached for our standard painkiller and made a joke of it.

"Whatever happens, I'll always think of you as the Boy at the Grave Next Door," I said. "You know, like in magazine stories. The boy who lives next door. That really nice chap the heroine grew up with. She doesn't realize how nice he is until she's been given the push by some Romeo in the city. Then she goes back home and settles down with the boy next door who's been waiting faithfully.

"Whatever happens to us, I want to come back to the Boy at the Grave Next Door when the time comes. To you, Benny. And then we can play pick-up-sticks with our bones until no one knows which bits are you and which are me. Will you wait faithfully?"

Benny sat quiet for a little while.

"Not if I can help it," he said. "And what are we going to do about the husbands and wives we pick up as we go through our lives?"

"We won't bother about them. Because it's you and me, Benny, even if it doesn't happen in this life."

"If some woman should ever decide to make an honest

man of me, I won't let her down," he said. "I'll want her in there with us."

We sat in silence for quite a while.

"Maybe it would be best if we didn't see each other any more," Benny said.

Just then, I was relieved he was taking some kind of decision for the pair of us. It didn't really sink in that this was the end. So I agreed.

He got up and took me by the hand. We moved so we were between our two gravestones. We put our arms around each other and stood quietly for a long time, maybe half an hour.

"Let's meet right here," I said finally. "In fifty years or so."

"See you!" he said sadly. And then he went.

I stayed there for a few moments, then I went home.

Don't suppose I'll ever know if Desirée realized I meant it seriously, that last time in the cemetery. Or how she took it, if so. What I think now is that she would quite happily have carried on the way we were—throwing herself into her job all week, then allowing herself a few hours of rural relaxation. Seeing it was always me coming to her, cap in hand, asking for more, it was odd that I was the one to bring matters to a head and break it off with her—at least, I think it was me. I couldn't go on like that; the price was too high. But breaking up with her almost did me in.

As soon as I got back from the cemetery, I kicked off my boots, went into the sitting room, and scrabbled around for a pen and pad in the bureau. Then I did a circuit of the farm. Went around like a building site inspector writing down everything that needed doing. I had my personal stereo on the whole time, blasting out Energy Radio at top volume, perfect for lobotomizing yourself for a while without doing any lasting damage. I set myself three jobs a day, on top of all the routine ones. And they were things like concreting a new manure base and building a new shed for the pump . . .

And I did it. Doggedly, I numbed myself with work, so much work I didn't even get time to read the local paper. I scarcely knew what day of the week it was. I'd go out at half past five every morning and be on the go until about ten at night. Then I'd come in and collapse; often I didn't even make it upstairs. There were days when I couldn't even remember if I'd had anything to eat.

I stuck at it until spring came and I had to get out into the fields. If the cows gave me even the slightest bother, they got a good dose of my boot, steel toe cap and all. One cow got so nervous I eventually had to fit a restraint to stop her kicking me. I thought they should be bloody grateful.

I didn't ever slip back into that apathy I was feeling before I met Shrimp. There was some kind of logical train of thought there: I'd given up the most tremendous thing in my life, for this. So I had to make a go of it. Give it all I'd got.

Then I went through a phase of thinking I ought to go out on a Saturday night. It was a job I set myself, like all the rest—get out there and size up what the market had to offer, same as at an agricultural machinery show. I went to the barber's and they did what they could with hair frayed like old rope; I put on a clean shirt and jeans and an old leather jacket. I hung around in pubs and chatted up girls, and since I didn't give a toss what they thought of me, it worked much better than my Smarmy Benny approach. I even brought one or two home with me, just as one-night stands. It was no consolation whatsoever; they never even had faces as far as I was concerned. But I can't honestly say it made me more depressed, either. There were women to be had, at any rate.

Then I stopped because I had all the spring plowing and sowing to get through. At that stage I was working eighteen hours a day, and one morning when I fainted in the boiler room, I realized something would have to give. I'd lost seven kilos in weight and I was having serious gastric problems. Thinking I'd at least get that sorted out, I rang Anita, and she came around one evening. When she saw me, she clapped her hands over her mouth. "I don't want to talk about it," I said. "Just give me the medicine."

A week later, she took her annual leave from work. "They're always pleased at the hospital if people can take it at different times, not in the summer," she said. She moved into Mum's room. She cooked boiled fish and soothing soups that were kind to my stomach, and massaged my back when I'd been out plowing on the tractor until eleven at night. She stocked up the fridge and freezer and cleaned and tidied the house; she put up some kitchen curtains and came out to the cowshed with me when I had to do the test milking. In the evenings she'd sit knitting while I read the *Farmer* and we didn't say much to start with.

It was like taking two aspirin when your head's about to burst. The pain slowly fades to a dull ache you can live with.

By the third week, I started telling her about it. She didn't say much, just nodded and kept an eye on her stitches. That was a blessing; if she'd started telling me what she thought of Shrimp, I'd have broken down.

By the fourth week, she moved into my bed with me. It wasn't so much a full string orchestra, more like a sauna when you're really stiff and clogged with dirt. Pleasant and natural but nothing to make you giddy with desire.

190

I didn't ring Desirée even once, and I avoided the ceme-tery. My parents would have understood.

A couple of times, not long after we split up, the tele-phone rang in the night. I knew who it was but I didn't pick up the receiver. I'd have been right back in it if I had.

I have to get through the minutes
one at a time,
swallow them like bitter pills,
try not to dwell on
the vast number still left

Everyone creates their own hell out of what they hate most. For the people around the Mediterranean, hell was perpetual heat; for those in the north, it was a realm of icy cold and silence.

I constructed my personal hell by letting all the mistakes I've made and all the opportunities I've missed pass before my eyes, like watching a film.

A week after Benny and I said good-bye in the cemetery, I knew he really meant it. It took me that long. I rang him one night to keep at least a tiny thread of contact going. He didn't answer and I knew he was making himself unavailable.

That was when the film started. First, it went through everything we said, that day he showed me his plans for the house. The more I replayed it, the more I thought I sounded like Donald Duck—a ghastly, self-satisfied Donald Duck quacking on and knowing it all. Saying "we" needed to prioritize and adapt, but meaning he needed to adapt to me. Thinking every possible solution must involve him sacrificing something—if I thought at all. And all the time convinced I was the great object of desire, the one who could make the choice. Only a couple of weeks ago, I'd been so worried because I didn't know what I wanted, or what I'd be prepared to give up—most likely nothing at all.

Of course Inez had warned me: "You were different. I've never seen you like that before." That had been a unique feeling, and she'd seen it but I hadn't. And that feeling now hit me with such a vengeance I was obliged to take two weeks' sick leave.

The first time I've been off sick since leaving school. I went to the shops for yogurt, bread, and eggs, and tottered home. Didn't go out, unplugged the phone, and plugged it back in again, several times a day. Replayed my film.

I remember those weeks mainly for the wild mood swings. One minute I was furious with Benny—he'd bloody well had no intention of giving up a single thing in his life, either. I was to move in with him, more or less give up my job, be adaptable to the point of letting Violet look after my child. I couldn't think of a single thing he'd sacrificed—his only concession had been redecorating his bedroom, and he hadn't even asked my advice before he did it. Willful. Stubborn. Demanding.

That night I rang to tell him what I thought of him. He still wasn't answering. Damn him.

The next moment I crept over to the mirror and saw my tear-stained face. Crying does nothing to improve the looks of people like me—red and swollen, with white lashes. I was horribly ugly—nobody else would ever see in me what Benny had seen. And shown me. He'd made me beautiful, and now the spell was broken.

That night I rang to cry on the phone and beg for mercy. I didn't even wait to hear if he answered before slamming down the receiver—good grief, I was turning into Sten, slurring and sniveling!

That was the last time I rang his number. But the wild mood swings went on. Sometimes I'd conjure up a sequence of images of him in my mind: in his forest owner's cap, slurping soup and spouting reactionary clichés. And then a sequence with him against the light, sitting laughing on the steps of Rowan Farm, his troll's hair all disheveled, stroking a cat on his lap. His sinewy arms pitchforking hay into huge stacks. And then I'd cry some more and write incessantly in my blue book. Depending which phase I was in, I either plugged in or unplugged the phone, waiting for the rings that I knew would never come.

I remember, too, how there seemed to be a vast number of minutes in every hour, and every minute passed very slowly. I was constantly looking at the clock. And I could hardly even get my yogurt down. One day I held my nose and swallowed three raw eggs in a row, because I got it into my head I was undernourished. The rest of the time I lived on clear soup.

It was much, much worse than anything I'd ever known before, worse than when Örjan died. I couldn't even summon the energy to feel ashamed of that. Örjan was as if expunged from my memory.

Märta could have helped me through those first days, but she was at a convalescent home in Småland. And after all, what had happened to her was so much more appalling, if you can have degrees of hell.

So then I cried for Märta, too.

At the end of two weeks, I dragged myself back to work. The others thought I'd had a bad dose of flu. Only Olof had seen my doctor's certificate. He said I was welcome to go and talk to him if I wanted, and I realized I'd be able to, now. But I didn't.

I buried myself in my job. It went well. It was really only when I was fully occupied that I felt more or less normal. As soon as I got home, or found myself sitting on my own for lunch, I felt as if my face was coming loose. As if it was made of Lego and could be taken to bits at any moment. And naturally, I couldn't sleep at nights. That's when I lay there going over all those missed opportunities. New ones every night. More and more of them.

When I was in town the other day, I saw Desirée for the first time since we split up. It had turned warm, and she was sitting at an outdoor café with a thin gray-haired guy. They were leaning toward each other and seemed engrossed in their conversation. There was a pile of books on the table. I passed so close by, I could see the top one was in English. Of course. Desirée was wearing lipstick and a stylish new jacket, bright blue. Her hair was longer than usual and a bit wavy. The gray-haired guy was laughing.

I wanted to kick his front teeth in. He didn't look as if he'd put up a fight. If Desirée had given him her summer holiday smile, in all likelihood I'd have jumped over the fence and gone crashing in between them. But she didn't.

When Anita's annual leave was over, she cut down her shifts by half, without even asking me about it. We carried on as we had been, and I taught her to drive the tractor so she could pack the silo when I was getting in the silage. We got the bikes out and started going on little excursions with a flask of coffee and a bite to eat; for Friday nights she'd rent a video (just one!) and buy some wine.

The first video she got out was *Police Academy*, by the way.

Whenever I was on my own, I'd have my personal stereo blaring. In the back of my mind I started seeing a new Desirée, with makeup and nice clothes and a series of guys who'd seen the world and liked reading books in English. So I suppose she'd got what she wanted!

And so had I, after all.

I wondered if she ever thought about me. And what she'd wanted, those times when she rang in the middle of the night. To shout at me for something, I expect.

I'd have liked to be sitting there opposite her, laughing and telling her how lovely she looked in lipstick, and in that new jacket. Seeing her smile.

But I'd made a decision and now it looks as if it won't have to be either / or: I can have the farm and a family.

With Anita. I guess that's how it's going to be and there are certainly worse things.

I don't think I ever really believed the thing I had with Shrimp could have a future. There was something disturbing about those intense feelings she gave me, and apparently still does give me—like wanting to kick in the teeth of a complete stranger! Anyway, I've never been much of a believer in "marrying for love," those relationships that start with you drowning in cleavage at a dance. Then, if the cleavage is the right age and unattached, you move on to all the usual mating rituals like seeing a film, family dinners, Ikea, and a holiday on Rhodes, and then you book the local church and it all runs like clockwork right through to the marriage guidance counseling.

I'm sure things worked just as smoothly when your parents chose your wife for you; at least you knew she'd be someone who'd suit you reasonably well, and then you just had to get used to her because there wouldn't be anyone else on offer. Mum could easily have chosen Anita.

I think both Anita and I sense we've passed our sell-by date where romance is concerned. We both need this; we can deprive the world of a middle-aged spinster and an aging bachelor to laugh at.

"Now she's an entirely different kettle of fish!" said Violet once she'd met Anita. Bengt-Göran knew her from before.

I went out and punched my fist hard against the porch. But then I went back in again.

Anita isn't stupid and she isn't dull, even though she doesn't make me laugh like Shrimp. I've always liked Anita and got on well with her. But I can't suddenly make myself fall in love with her, any more than I can start warbling operatic arias. I just haven't got it in me.

And she'd never ask me if I "love" her.

People love cats and strawberry ice cream and polo-neck sweaters and Ibiza—and then all of a sudden they're supposed to "love" one single person until they stop doing that and start "loving" someone else. On a par with a game of spin the bottle, I've always thought.

It's like that old joke about the stork—I don't believe in the stork, although I've seen one myself.

I don't believe in Love, although I've experienced it. I could say. When I can't sleep, I lie there imagining it's because I never actually gave it a chance. I kind of never reached the stage of thinking I had to put it first, in front of everything else.

Sometimes I feel I haven't really reached dry land yet, and maybe never will.

When my thoughts go skidding off to the idea of starting a family, for example, I can't help thinking of Shrimp, pregnant, with my baby like a ball in that thin white body. Of making her pregnant. Like she longed to be.

I can understand why people's brains short-circuit and repress all memory of it after they think they've had an encounter with aliens. They just can't accommodate it in their picture of the world; they have to rebuild everything from scratch. And believe me, I shall repress Shrimp to the point where I can't even find my way to the library.

Mending burst soap bubbles
and making dolls with sleeping eyes smile
takes time

I dreamed I was in a shoe shop at sale time. In a pile of shoes on a table, I found a gorgeous blue leather shoe, all strappy; it was a right shoe, and I put it on my foot. In real life, my legs are as white and sticklike as rounders bats, but in my dream that shoe made my right leg look shapely and silky brown, my ankle as graceful as a ballerina's. So I started hunting for the left shoe. When I found it, it was tiny, the size that would fit a five-year-old. "That happens sometimes," said the shop assistant, unconcerned. "Take them or leave them. They're the only pair we've got." But how could I buy an odd pair of shoes like that? Chop off half my foot? I left the shop regretfully, and then I woke up.

I forced myself to think of that dream whenever my thoughts strayed in Benny's direction. Half my foot.

It was part of my rehabilitation, however, to change the way I looked. I started by applying a little mascara to disguise my swollen eyes, and powder to hide the dark

200

rings. Then I moved on to lipstick, and I realized it felt good, becoming more visible in men's eyes. Every time somebody's eyes lingered on me, it felt like a little dose of revenge on Benny: see, there is somebody who wants me, after all! Then I bought a few new clothes in bright colors, mainly to convince myself I was alive. I succeeded quite well.

In May the library sent me on a two-week course down in Lund. I popped over to Copenhagen and went to the Glyptotek. In the entrance hall they've got that statue of Niobe with her children crawling all over her. I took pictures from every possible angle. Then I spent hours in the gallery of busts of Roman emperors and empresses. By about AD 200–300, they start to look as sharp and realistic as photographs, and you can chart a single person's looks from childhood to old age.

How will I look in fifty years' time? And Benny?

I promised myself I'd look him up when I was eighty, come what may. He could scarcely refuse me that.

In my summer holidays I signed up for a course in watercolor painting on the west coast of Ireland. We sat all day long with the gulls shrieking around us, trying to capture the glint of the sun on the water at the base of the cliffs. An American couple, brother and sister, invited me to Wisconsin for Christmas. He was a college lecturer and very pleasant to sit in silence with.

In a dusty little pub in Ballylaoghaire I saw an old fridge like the one Benny has in his kitchen. Or had? It might all be different now.

Once, just once, I borrowed a car and drove through the village where Benny's farm is. I persuaded myself I was on the way to pick wild raspberries in the big clearing in the woods near the next village. And on the way I saw Benny and a dark-haired, suntanned woman. There they were, cycling toward me with picnic things in their bike baskets, but they didn't notice me in the car, of course. Benny seemed to be explaining something and pointing out over the fields. He was slim and tanned and had his hair cut a different way. He looked happy.

As for her, she looked rather drab. Good company for Violet, I thought. And then I began to wonder whether he makes love to her the same way he did to me, and then I couldn't bear it any longer and hardly made it home, and swore I'd never go there again.

Märta was more and more her old self—on the surface. But she put me in mind of a toy I had as a child, a yellow tin duck that could waddle on its flat feet and go quack when you wound it up with a key. One day I wound it too far and the spring broke. I just couldn't accept that it would never go again: it looked the same on the outside.

Märta's spring had broken.

But the difference between human beings and tin ducks is, among other things, that our springs can heal, given time. Märta met a man in a wheelchair. He'd had a colostomy, and was irascible and moody. "There you go!" said Märta. "At least with him, I always know where he's got to!" His life certainly got a lot more adventurous after he met her. She insisted wheelchair users can do everything the rest of us can, then lost hold of the chair on a steep slope when she'd taken him out hill walking. The chair tipped over and he cursed her, but she simply shook herself and dragged him up another hill.

In September I started my storytime sessions again. A little blond boy with brown eyes would often sit right at the front and interrupt the story with suggestions on ways to improve it. His dad would sit over by the wall looking proud and embarrassed. They stayed behind afterward once, to talk, and I went with them to a café. The dad's name is Anders and he lives alone with his little boy. We started meeting up for outings or museum visits, or cooked dinner for each other. Anders is a historian and talks about the past in such entertainingly irreverent terms that I don't know what to believe, but he often makes me laugh.

I hoped I might be falling in love with him.

One day, when all three of us were out for a walk in the park, his little Daniel, lower lip quivering, came out with: "I feel sorry for eagles!"

"Why's that?" Anders asked.

"Because they can't get into nesting boxes."

It was then I realized it was Daniel I was in love with.

In October, an everyday miracle happened. In a shop window I saw a gorgeous pair of strappy, blue leather shoes. I recognized them. I went straight in and bought them, wore them home, and made a phone call the minute I got in.

I thought I understood about miracles.
They were my job. Sowing and reaping life.
But you never know where you are with miracles.
They creep up on you from behind and grab you
by the scruff of the neck.

Anita wants us to get engaged.

"I can't, I've got no ring finger on my left hand!" I said. But then I stopped wriggling. It was only fair.

Then suddenly, one evening in October, Shrimp rang. I'd just come in from the cowshed; Anita was in the kitchen with some pork chops sizzling in the pan. Energy Radio was pounding away.

I swapped to the other phone and went up to the bed-room.

"Yes?"

"Can you come to my place? Right away? Nothing terrible's happened, it's just that I've got to talk to you about something."

"Now? This evening's not very convenient. Tomorrow?"

I tried to sound unbothered, but I wasn't, of course. Bothered?

It went quiet for a bit.

"No," she said. "This evening or not at all. But I won't be angry if you don't come. It's perfectly all right."

"I'll be there in half an hour," I said.

Anita didn't ask why I'd got to go into town all of a sudden. But she wondered, I'm sure. I usually tell her where I'm going.

I didn't think at all on the way in. Just drummed my fingers on the steering wheel and tried to empty my head of thought.

She let me in with her face set strictly to neutral and asked me to sit down in her uncomfortable tubular steel armchair. She was just the same, and yet she wasn't. Whose doing was it that she'd started to wear makeup? She had the usual pale-colored clothes, jeans and a sweater, but peculiarly enough also a really smart pair of blue shoes with straps.

She took a seat opposite me, with the look of a child counting down to a jump into cold water: ten, nine, eight, seven, six . . . A moment's silence, then we both started talking at once.

We laughed, a bit uneasily. She looked at me and I've seldom seen her looking so affectionate. I can't recall her looking like that very often.

"I couldn't wait fifty years, though that was my original plan," she said. "Don't worry. I've no intention of messing up your life. But there's one thing I want to ask you, and I don't know how to start."

"You could always turn it into a joke. That's what you

used to do when I was trying to be serious," I said, and I could hear how bitter I sounded. Below the belt! After all, I'd been the same myself. I had to take the edge off it, somehow.

"Read anything good recently?" I asked. That was one of the old catchphrases that generally got us going. She'd answer something like "Schopenhauer" and I'd say *The Phantom Christmas Annual*, and then we'd compare them. "Schopenhauer's worldview is consistently worked through!—Yes, but the Phantom's got much cooler underpants . . ." That sort of routine had been our salvation many a time when we'd ventured onto thin ice. And sometimes we'd managed to get some serious things said by kind of wrapping them up in the banter.

"The other day I read about a scientific investigation in France," she said. "They got a load of men to sleep in new white pants and sweat into them; then they got a load of women to smell the underwear and choose which man they were most interested in. It turned out that every single one chose the man whose immune defenses complemented their own. So their offspring would be healthy, in other words."

"So it was my immune defenses that turned you on, not the farm?"

"Who knows?"

She lapsed into silence and looked as if she was counting again: five, four, three, two, one—go!

"This is what I want. I've wanted it all along and I don't know why. What I mean is, I want a baby with you. No, let me finish! I don't mean I want us to start all over again. I just need to make this bloody biological clock shut up, or

I'm not going to get anywhere. Those little eggs I feel so chock-full of, I want to give them a chance, just one. And you needn't know a thing."

"Are you planning to knock me out and assault me?" I said. I admit I was gaping at her, openmouthed.

"My idea is to ask you to come to bed with me one last time," she said, regarding me gravely. "Now, while they're really jumping around. And it's got to be right now. You seem to be the only one who really gets them going."

My whole life passed before my eyes, as they say.

"And then you needn't hear another word about it. Unless you absolutely insist, of course. And it's not going to work—there's no way it'll work—but at least I'll have tried, and then I can stop thinking about it and we can both go off and live happily ever after, in our two separate worlds." She stole a look at my ring.

I said nothing.

"It'd certainly have one hell of an immune defense system," she mumbled. "No, forget I said that! I've never been more deadly earnest than now. I think I'd put 'father unknown' on the form. Don't say a word! I haven't thought it all through, for obvious reasons. And there are other considerations, I know, I know! So I'm going to give you an hour to think it over. I'll leave you to it."

She leaped up, grabbed her fabric bag, and headed for the door.

"If you're not here when I get back, I'll know. At least I'll have done what I could, and they'll have to start jumping for somebody else . . . But I'll always remember you as my very best playmate. Though I shan't think of you all that often."

She slipped out before I had a chance to say a word.

I must have looked the way the cows do when the emergency slaughterman fires the stun gun.

I looked around me. The shell poster was gone. In its place was a watercolor painting of some cliffs and the sea, and a blown-up photo of some statue, a fat woman with a mob of kids crawling all over her.

If I went along with her crazy proposal, I'd be doing the same to Anita as that Robertino did to her friend Märta. It was out of the question. I sat there for forty-nine minutes, chewing my empty knuckles. Then I disengaged my brain and switched to autopilot.

She threw down her bag in the hall and came rushing in. At first she didn't see me, because it had got dark and I hadn't put a light on. She switched on the ceiling light, saw I was there and started crying, and pretty soon her mascara was running.

"Oh no!" I said. "You needn't think I'm leaving all the decisions to you! I've got conditions, too. Firstly, none of this 'father unknown' nonsense. What d'you think I am, a deadbeat? You'd turn my lad into some down-at-heel university lecturer in dead languages. Secondly, I want three goes—that's what they always get in fairy tales. I come here twice more—tomorrow and the day after. And you don't go with anybody else in the meantime, and neither do I, of course. After the third time, I go home and mind my own business and you stay here and we don't hear from each other until you ring. By then, you've either got a period or a test result."

"Even so, we've only got a one-in-five chance," she sniffed.

"Think I don't know how tricky it is, getting heifers

pregnant?" I said. It was a hell of a struggle getting my words out; they were slurring all over the place. "But at least you won't be sent straight to the abattoir if it doesn't work. If it does work, we'll teach it the soprano part of the *Messiah*. And if it doesn't, I promise to be deliriously happy without you, and every time I go to the library I'll come by your desk and slap you on the back. You can imagine how often that'll be."

We held hands and went into her white bedroom.

There's no way of describing how it felt, at least not this side of the Nobel Prize for literature.

And when I came back to my senses, I knew I still had two attempts left. Though in fairy tales they always fail the first two. Then some mysterious little man in gray pops up and tells them the magic words.

I'll be keeping my eyes peeled for that little devil.

A PENGUIN READERS GUIDE TO

BENNY & SHRIMP

———————————

Katarina Mazetti

An Introduction to
Benny & Shrimp

A man and a woman, both of them lonely, meet and fall in love. Both of them crave companionship and family; both are intelligent and good-humored. As Benny and Desirée (a.k.a. Shrimp) are about to discover, all that can stand between them and happiness is—everything.

Benny is a dairy farmer struggling to keep his late parents' farm alive in a modern world. Desirée is a small-town librarian who has retreated even further into her shell after the death of her young husband. They live in Sweden, and their love story begins surprisingly enough in a cemetery: it is there, visiting their loved ones' graves, that they first spot each other. Their differences are obvious immediately—she's appalled by the tacky decorations he so carefully arranges around his mother's grave and he's turned off by her peaked bookworm looks—but lust and longing drive them into each other's arms. Just when it looks like love could conquer all, reality rears its ugly head with a vengeance. How can Desirée (whom Benny promptly nicknames "Shrimp"), with her love of high culture, independence, and postmodern theory, be happy in a creaking old farmhouse that's stuck in the 1950s? And how can a man like Benny, who sings to his cows on Christmas Eve and longs for a buxom woman to come along and help run the farm, reconcile himself to store-bought meatballs and evenings at the opera?

In *Benny & Shrimp*, Katarina Mazetti allows her two characters to speak for themselves in alternating chapters, giving readers an intimate look inside the minds of two people as they struggle to bridge the gap between their separate worlds for the sake of true love. The farmer and the librarian could be two figures in a pastoral fable, but here they spring to life in all their sexy, infuriating, confounding messiness. Will modern-day practicality keep them apart, or will the unlikely couple live the fairy-tale ending? Either way, their path is a universal one of love, heartbreak, and hope.

ABOUT KATARINA MAZETTI

Katarina Mazetti began her career as a teacher and later moved into broadcast journalism. She is a prize-nominated author, commentator, musician, poet, and the producer of *Freja*, a program for women on Swedish radio. *Benny & Shrimp* has sold more than 450,000 copies in her native Sweden.

A CONVERSATION WITH KATARINA MAZETTI

What was the original seed or inspiration for this story?

Actually, a funeral. I was living on a farm at the time, married to a farmer. One of our neighbors died a horrible death, crushed under a tractor. It was a tragic funeral, but I knew that his wife had been considering divorce. I wondered if you can really feel grief for someone you are about to leave, or if you would fake it.

One day at work I was expecting a phone call from abroad and could not leave my desk. Slowly I started writing a short story about a woman who is ashamed that she cannot grieve for her husband properly. Suddenly, there was this man sitting on a bench nearby on the cemetery. . . . And the book started writing itself.

I think the man entered the story somehow because I was getting more and more annoyed that town people know so little about the hard work of farming and ask stupid questions like: "So tell me—what do farmers do during the winter?" As if dairy cows go into hibernation!

Each chapter begins with a bit of poetry taken from Desirée's notebook. You're a poet yourself; did you begin this story with the poems, or did they come later? How difficult was it to write poetry in Desirée's voice as opposed to prose?

Actually, like Desirée, I am quite a mediocre poet but I am willing to fight for everyone's right to write even bad poetry! But neither Desirée nor I really had any plans to publish; writing it is really more a state of mind, a relief, a consolation, or a way to cope with everyday life and need not be published. Excellent poetry would really have been out of place here.

Did you do a lot of research about the daily lives of Swedish dairy farmers? Do you have a personal connection to farming yourself?

Yes. I lived on a small dairy farm in the north of Sweden for nearly twenty years while working as a radio producer. But the book is not really autobiographical—like most books, it is a compost, "decomposed remnants of organic matter" of experiences and ideas.

Benny and Shrimp each seem like real, complex individuals, while at the same time they are representatives of certain "types," the taciturn farmer and the bluestocking librarian. Are either of these characters based on people you've met?

All the characters are of course based on people I've met, sometimes in the mirror.

Desirée's ambivalence about her husband's death and her real feelings for him might come across as rather unsentimental to American readers. Do you think there are cultural differences in how the emotions of characters (particularly female characters) in novels are portrayed? Or is this ambivalence unique to Desirée?

Desirée does her best to be a good wife and to grieve properly for her husband—would American readers really blame her that she can't? Do they think feelings can be strictly controlled? (That is not the impression you get from reading great American literature.) But in a general sense—yes. I do think there are cultural differences in what emotions readers expect from characters in a book. (Russian men, for example, tend to find this book horrifyingly feminist!) Though in most cultures women are expected to be more sentimental and softhearted than men, I find that in real life, men are often the more sentimental ones.

Desirée's library colleague Inez has an unusual role to play in this love story—how and why did you develop her character and her impact on Desirée?

I am glad that you asked that question! Inez is really my favorite character—a spectator, someone who watches human life like a bird-watcher—she does not really feel she is a participant but she finds it very interesting. And she has no hidden agenda. This makes her a reliable observer, not in the least sentimental. Desirée feels this and trusts her judgment. I have met Inezes, though they are quite rare. I should like to become one myself one day.

You write from the perspective of both the man and the woman in this love story. How did you, as a woman, get yourself inside Benny's head in order to portray him so realistically? Is there a stereotype of the "bachelor farmer" in Sweden that you were playing with?

One of the things that has amused me very much is that male readers often ask me who has helped me with "the Benny bit." "That is exactly how guys think," they say. But I have had no expert male to help me, I just tried to imagine how I myself would feel and act in Benny's situation, being reared in a certain gender tradition. (Something like what Flaubert might have meant when he said, "Madame Bovary, c'est moi!") Their reaction tells me, though, that there is no real difference between how men and women think, it is all a matter of upbringing. (Simone de Beauvoir would have agreed.)

Did you struggle with how to end the story, or did you always have this particular ending in mind?

The whole book was more like a rodeo! I tried to stay in control but toward the end, it got out of hand. And suddenly it was all over. (That's why I felt I had to write a sequel, which I did a few years later.)

QUESTIONS FOR DISCUSSION

Visit www.penguin.com to begin the discussion with online commentary by the author.

1. *Benny & Shrimp* presents some hard truths about modern relationships in a fairy-tale-like setting (or maybe it's the other way around). What are some themes, characters or images that seem to come from fairy tales and what seems distinctly twenty-first century to you?

2. Of all the seemingly irresolvable conflicts that Benny and Desirée encounter, which did you have the most sympathy for and which seemed unimportant to you?

3. Do you think one of them should compromise more than the other to make a life together work? If so, which one?

4. Is it surprising to you that the barriers between Benny and Desirée are issues of class, money, and education, considering that the story is set in the present and in a country (Sweden) that is thought by many to be particularly egalitarian?

5. Desirée's colleague Inez archives the lives of the people around her. What does she represent to you in this story? Do her archives or her peculiar use of them symbolize something to you?

6. Marta, Desirée's best friend, seems to be playing out an operatic version of Benny and Desirée's own love story in the wings. How does the relationship of the two title characters compare to that of Marta's with her "Grand Passion"?

7. Both Benny and Desirée were deeply influenced, though in very different ways, by their parents. (For examples, see pages 55–56 and 95–98.) How do those influences play out in their relationship? How aware do you think they are of those influences and their effects?

8. Benny and Desirée's attraction for each other starts off as primarily (and strongly) sexual, as opposed to Desiree's relationship with Orjan or Benny's with Anita. How do you think this beginning affects the way their relationship unfolds?

9. What did you think of the ending? What do you hope or imagine will happen to these two characters in their future?

For more information about or to order other Penguin Readers Guides, please e-mail the Penguin Marketing Department at reading@us.penguingroup.com or write to us at:

> Penguin Books Marketing Dept.
> Readers Guides
> 375 Hudson Street
> New York, NY 10014-3657

Please allow 4–6 weeks for delivery.
To access Penguin Readers Guides online, visit the Penguin Group (USA) Inc. Web sites at www.penguin.com and www.vpbookclub.com.

WITHDRAWN